"Engaged."

Her mother said the word again, as if savoring it, and smiled. "Oh, Naomi, you're marrying Toby McKittrick. It's just wonderful."

Naomi had never been on the receiving end of that smile before, so it threw her a little. Then she realized exactly what her mother had said. She wasn't thrilled about the baby, but about her daughter marrying Toby. Handsome. Stable. *Wealthy* Toby McKittrick. That was the kind of announcement her mother could get behind.

And that realization only made Naomi furious. At Toby. She hadn't expected her parents to be supportive, but having Toby ride to the rescue felt, after that first burst of relief, more than a little annoying. She'd only wanted him here for moral support. Not to sweep in and lie to save her. The whole purpose of coming here to tell her parents the truth was to get it over with.

"Toby—"

He looked down at her, gave her a smile, then surprised her into being quiet with a quick, hard kiss that left her lips buzzing. Shock rattled her. He'd never kissed her before, and though it wasn't a lover's kiss, it wasn't exactly a brotherly kiss, either.

* * *

A Texas-Sized Secret is part of the series
Texas Cattleman's Club: Blackmail—

No secret—or heart—is safe in Royal, Texas...

Dear Reader,

This time, I was lucky enough to be asked to write two of the books in the Texas Cattleman's Club continuity, so I was able to spend a lot of time in Royal, Texas. And I enjoyed every bit of it!

In this book, *A Texas-Sized Secret*, you'll meet Toby McKittrick, who built his fortune with his inventions and now indulges his love for raising horses on his ranch. He's got everything he ever wanted, until his best friend, Naomi Price, shows up with a problem.

Naomi was raised by parents who barely noticed her existence, so she's spent a lifetime trying to win approval that was never going to happen. Then she discovers that she's pregnant from one night with the wrong man, *and* that the Royal blackmailer knows all about it. He's going to tell the world, so she has to break it to her parents first.

Toby won't let her take the heat alone, though, and instead tells everyone that he is the baby's father. They agree to a marriage of convenience, but there's nothing convenient about Toby's new feelings for his best friend.

Naomi and Toby have to find a way through the gossip—and toward each other.

I really hope you enjoy this trip back to Royal as much as I did!

Happy Reading!

Maureen Child

MAUREEN CHILD

A TEXAS-SIZED SECRET

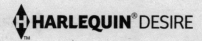

HARLEQUIN® DESIRE

Special thanks and acknowledgment are given to Maureen Child for her contribution to the Texas Cattleman's Club: Blackmail miniseries.

Recycling programs for this product may not exist in your area.

ISBN-13: 978-0-373-83849-3

A Texas-Sized Secret

Printed in U.S.A.

Maureen Child writes for the Harlequin Desire line and can't imagine a better job. A seven-time finalist for a prestigious Romance Writers of America RITA® Award, Maureen is an author of more than one hundred romance novels. Her books regularly appear on bestseller lists and have won several awards, including a Prism Award, a National Readers' Choice Award, a Colorado Romance Writers Award of Excellence and a Golden Quill Award. She is a native Californian but has recently moved to the mountains of Utah.

Visit her Author Profile page at Harlequin.com, or maureenchild.com, for more titles.

To the readers, because you are the reason
we have stories to tell.

One

"What did I ever do to this Maverick?" Naomi Price kicked at the dirt, then gave a heavy sigh. "Why's he after me?"

Toby McKittrick glanced from the horse he was saddling to the woman standing on the other side of the corral fence. Even furious and a little scared, Naomi made quite the picture.

She was nine inches shorter than his own six feet two inches, but she had a lot of interest packed into her five-foot-five frame. Her long, copper-brown hair draped over her shoulders like fire, and her chocolate-colored eyes snapped with intelligence and, at the moment, worry. She wore white summer slacks and a loose, pale green shirt with some white lacy thing over it. The boots she wore were ankle-high, pale cream and fit only for walking down clean city sidewalks. Here on the ranch, they'd be ruined in a day or two. But Naomi was a city girl, so no worries.

"This Maverick," he said, "he—or *she*, for all we know," Toby pointed out, "is after everybody, it seems. Guess it was just your turn."

"Maverick" had been creating turmoil in Royal, Texas, for the last few months. Exposing private bombshells, taunting people with their innermost worries and fears, whoever it was not only knew the people of Royal, but didn't give a good damn about them.

Somehow this person—whoever—uncovered people's darkest secrets and then published them. Toby had no idea what the mysterious Maverick was getting out of all this— okay, some people had paid Maverick to keep his mouth shut—but Toby had the feeling the whole point was simply to try to destroy people's reputations. If that was it, he was batting a thousand.

"Great," Naomi muttered. "Just great."

"What exactly did he say to get you running out here first thing in the morning?" Toby gave her a long look. Usually, Naomi wasn't up and moving until the crack of noon. She didn't go anywhere unless she was completely turned out from the top of her head to the toes of her stylish shoes.

She sighed, then reached into her shoulder bag for her cell phone. "Look at it for yourself," she said, handing it over.

Toby gave the horse a pat, took the phone and keyed it up.

"It's ready to go," she said, "just push Play."

Frowning, Toby tipped the brim of his hat back and tapped the phone screen. Instantly, he saw what had Naomi as jumpy as a spider on a hot plate.

For the last year or so, Naomi had been the star, writer and producer of a small-town cable fashion show. She was making a name for herself, doing what she did best—advising women on how to look good. Naomi was proud of what she'd accomplished, and she had a right to be. She'd built herself an audience and she worked hard every day to put out the best show possible.

He scowled at the screen as the video played. Maverick had turned what she did into a parody. He'd found an actress who resembled Naomi to star in it, and the woman was cooing and sighing over a rack of dresses like she was having an orgasm on camera. Then she stepped out from behind that rack and Toby knew instantly what had *really* set Naomi off.

The actress looked about two years pregnant. She waddled across the stage, both hands supporting a belly so huge there might have been a baby elephant tucked inside.

"Oh, man…"

"Wait for it," Naomi ground out. "There's more."

A deep frown etched on his face, Toby watched and listened as the actress began talking with a slow, overblown Texas accent.

"And for summer," she said, simpering at the camera, "maternity wear just got more exciting! Our big ol' bellies won't keep us from looking stylish, ladies." She flipped long reddish-brown hair behind her shoulder, then rubbed both hands over that comically distended belly before slipping behind that rack of dresses again, still talking. "Remember, accessorizing is key. Drape a pretty belt around that baby belly. Draw attention to it. Be proud. Show the world what a fashionable pregnant woman should look like."

Toby's own temper was starting to spike for Naomi's sake.

She stepped out from behind the dress rack again to model an oversize tent dress with a gigantic black belt enveloping that belly. "Tell the world, Naomi," the woman said, smiling into the camera. "Do it fast, or Maverick will do it for you."

Gritting his teeth, Toby turned the phone off and handed it back to her. "Okay, I see what's got you all churned up."

She tucked her phone back into her purse and then reached out to grab the top rail of the corral fence. Her hands tightened on the weather-beaten wood until her knuckles went white.

"It's not just that he's threatening to tell everyone I'm pregnant, Toby," she said, her voice tight but low enough that he had to lean in to hear her. "It's that he's making fun of me. He's turning my show into a joke. He's *laughing* at me."

Toby laid his hand over one of hers and squeezed. "Doesn't matter what he thinks of you, Naomi. You know that."

"Of course I know," she said, giving him a grim smile that was brave, if not honest. "But I watched that video and wondered if I really sound like that. All know-it-all and prissy. Am I prissy?"

One corner of Toby's mouth quirked up. "I wouldn't say so, but you've had your moments…"

She looked at him for a long minute, then let her head fall back and a groan escape her throat. "You're talking about the mean girls thing, aren't you?"

He shrugged and went back to tightening the cinch on his horse's saddle. Naomi had been his best friend for years. But that didn't make him blind to her faults, either. Of course, *nobody* was perfect. Toby knew Naomi better than anyone else, and he knew that she had spent a lifetime hiding a tender heart beneath a self-protective layer of cool disdain.

"You, Simone and Cecelia have a reputation you more than earned. You've gotta admit that."

"Wish I didn't have to," she muttered and dropped her chin on top of her hands.

Shaking his head, Toby let her be, knowing her thoughts were racing. So were his own. Naomi and he had been best friends for years now. They'd grown up knowing each other in a vague, from-the-same-small-town kind of way. But in college, they'd connected when he was a senior and she a freshman. He knew her in a way not many people did, so Toby also knew that Naomi was shaken right down to her expensive, useless boots.

"Things are different now," Naomi insisted a moment later. She straightened up, and Toby was glad to see a fierce gleam in her eyes. "People change, you know."

"All the time," he said, nodding.

"Cecelia and Deacon are together now—she's pregnant, too," Naomi pointed out unnecessarily. "And Simone and Hutch have worked things out and she's pregnant with triplets, for heaven's sake." She threw up both hands and let them fall to her sides. "It's a population explosion with the three of us. We're not the mean girls anymore. We're..." She sighed. "I don't know what we are anymore."

"I do," Toby said, watching her with a smile. "You're Naomi Price—the woman who wears useless boots that cost more than my saddle..."

She laughed, as he'd meant her to.

Staring directly into her eyes, he continued. "You're also the woman who started her own television show and worked her behind off to make it a success."

"Thank you, Toby." She smiled at him, and he felt a sharp tug inside in response.

"Okay," she said, nodding to herself as she pushed away from the fence, giving that top rail one last slap. "You're right. I'm strong. I'm ready. I can do this."

"Yes, you can." Finished saddling his horse,

Toby stroked the flat of his hand along the animal's sleek neck.

"I don't know how to tell them," she said, all the air leaving her body in a rush. "The whole strong, independent feminist thing just goes right out the window when I know I have to face down my parents and tell them I'm pregnant."

Toby turned, braced his forearms on the top rail of the fence and tugged the brim of his dark brown hat down low over his eyes. "You should have already told them."

"This is so not the time for cool logic," she snapped. Pacing back and forth along the fence line, she crossed her arms over her middle like she was hugging herself. "What happened to Mr. Supportive?"

"I'm being supportive," he argued. "I'm just not patting your head, because you don't need it."

She muttered something he didn't quite catch and kept pacing. If she'd stop walking so damn fast, he'd give her a hug himself. But the minute he considered it, Toby pushed the thought aside. Hell, he'd been burying his attraction for Naomi for years. He was a damn expert. She'd come to his ranch looking for a friend, so that was what he'd be for her. Which meant telling her what she didn't want to hear.

"Naomi," he said, "you knew you couldn't keep this a secret forever."

She stopped directly opposite him, with the fence separating them. A soft summer wind lifted the ends of her hair, and she squinted a bit into the sunlight, those beautiful brown eyes of hers narrowing. "I know, but..."

"But nothing," he said, yanking his hat off to stab his fingers through his hair. "Somebody else took the reins from you. You don't have a choice now in when to tell your folks. Time's up."

"How did Maverick even find out?" She took a breath and exhaled on a heavy sigh. "You're the only one—or so I thought—besides me who knows about the baby."

That sounded like an accusation. His gaze snapped to hers. "I didn't tell anyone."

"I know that." She waved that away with such casualness he relaxed again. Toby was a man of his word. Always. The one thing he always remembered his father saying was, "Without his honor, a man's got nothing." That had always stuck with him, to the point that Toby never made a promise unless he was sure he could keep it.

"You know, you're the only man in my life who's never let me down, Toby," she said softly. "The one person I can always count on."

He nodded but didn't say anything, because knowing Naomi, she had more to say.

"I tried to contact Gio again."

And there it was. Irritation spiked inside him, and Toby didn't bother to hide it. Gio Fabiani, a one-night stand who had left Naomi pregnant and wasn't worth the dust on her fancy boots. But Naomi being

Naomi, for the last couple of months she'd been trying to track the man down to tell him about the baby. Even if she did finally find him, though, Toby was sure that Gio wouldn't give a flying damn.

"You've got to let that go," he ground out. "Just because the man fathered your child doesn't mean he's good enough to *be* its father."

"I know, but—"

"No buts," he said, interrupting her. "Damn it, Naomi, you told me yourself that sleeping with that sleaze was a mistake. You really want to make another one by bringing him back into your life?"

"Shouldn't he *know* that he has a child?"

"If he hadn't blown in and out of your life so fast, he *would* know," Toby said, though in truth he was damned grateful that Gio hadn't been more than a blip on Naomi's radar. She deserved better. "I did some checking of my own when you first told me about this."

"You checked? Into Gio?"

"Who else?" He calmed himself by stroking his palm up and down the length of his horse's neck. "The man's a worthless user. He goes through women like we go through feed for the horses."

She flushed, and he knew she didn't like hearing it, but true was true.

His voice low and soft, Toby added, "He's never going to stand with you, Naomi."

She took a breath and huffed it out again. "I know that, too. And I don't want him to, anyway." Shaking her head, she started pacing again. "One night of bad judgment doesn't make for a relationship. But I should tell him about the baby before this Maverick person sends that video out into the world and it goes viral." She stopped opposite him again and laid one hand against her belly. "Viral. People *everywhere* will see that awful video. People will be laughing at me. Feeling *sorry* for me. Or, worse, cheering, because like you said, I haven't always been the nicest human being on the planet. Oh, God, my stomach's churning and it has nothing to do with the baby."

"You'll survive this," he said.

"Why should I have to *survive*? Who *is* this Maverick? Why has nobody found him yet?"

"I don't know—to all those questions."

Shooting another speculative look at his friend, Toby wondered exactly what she was thinking. With Naomi it was never easy to guess. She'd long since learned to school her features into a blank mask that could convince her disinterested parents that all was well. But usually with him, she was more forthcoming. Still, things were different now. She was more shaken than he'd ever seen her. It wasn't just the pregnancy—it was how her life seemed to be spinning out of her control.

And Naomi liked control.

"The video he sent me was just…" Her sentence trailed off as she shook her head. "If he puts that out on the internet like he threatened, everyone in town's going to know my secret in a few hours."

Toby sighed, braced both forearms on the top rung of the corral fence and waited until her gaze met his to say, "Honey, they were all going to know within another month or two anyway. It's not like you could hide it much longer."

He was repeating himself and he knew it, but sometimes it took a hammer to pound the truth into Naomi's mind when she didn't want to admit to something. That hard head of hers was one of the things he liked most about her. Which made him a damn fool, probably. But there was something about the look she got in her eye when she was set on something that twisted his guts into knots. Knots he couldn't do a damn thing about, since she was his best friend. But he did wonder from time to time if Naomi's insides ever twisted over him.

Naomi stopped pacing, spun around to look at him and blurted, "You're right."

That surprised Toby enough that his eyebrows lifted high on his forehead. She saw it and laughed, and blast if the sound didn't light fires inside him. Fires he deliberately ignored. Hell, of course his body responded as it did. She was a beautiful woman with a laugh that sounded like warm nights and silk sheets. A man would have to be dead six months to not be affected by Naomi.

"I'm not so stubborn—or delusional—I can't see the truth when it takes a bite out of me," she said. Leaning her arms on the fence rail alongside his, she said, "That's really why I came out to see you this morning. I know what I have to do, and I wanted to ask you to come with me to tell my parents."

He frowned a little, because he didn't much care for Naomi's folks. They were always so prissy, so sure of their own righteousness they put him off. Their house was like a damn museum, quiet, still, where a dust speck wouldn't have the nerve to show up. Always made him feel like a clumsy cowboy.

But he knew how they made Naomi feel, too. She'd never quite measured up to parents who probably shouldn't have had a child to begin with. From everything Naomi had told him and from what he'd seen firsthand, they'd been showing her for years in word and deed just how disappointing she was to them. The announcement she had to make today wasn't going to help the situation any.

She was watching him, waiting for an answer, and Toby saw a flicker of unease in her eyes. He didn't like it. "Sure," he said, "I'll come along."

"Thanks, Toby," she said, reaching over to lay one hand on his forearm. "I knew you'd do this for me. You really are my best friend."

A best friend probably shouldn't experience a jolt of lust with just a touch of her hand on his arm. So he'd just keep that to himself.

Naomi was nervous. But then, she'd *been* nervous since opening the email with the subject line Your Secret Is Out. She'd known the moment she saw the blasted thing in her inbox that Maverick had finally turned his talons toward her. For the last few months, she'd watched as people she knew and cared about had had their lives turned upside down by this malicious phantom. And somehow she'd managed to keep hoping he wouldn't turn on her. Now that he had, though, she was forced to tell her parents the truth and live through what she always thought of as the "disappointment stare." Again.

Her entire life, Naomi had known that she was continually letting her parents down. Oh, no one had actually *said* anything—that would have been distasteful. But parents had other ways of letting their children know they didn't measure up, and the Prices were masters at silent disapproval.

No matter what Naomi had done in her life, her mother and father stood back and looked at her as if they didn't have a clue where she'd come from. Today was going to be no different.

Thank God Toby was coming with her to face them. She glanced at his stoic profile as he drove his Ford 150 down the road toward her family's mini mansion. He was the only one who knew her secret. The only one she'd trusted enough to go to when she realized two months ago that she was pregnant. And didn't that say something? She hadn't even told Cecelia Morgan and Simone Parker, and the three of them had been close for years.

But when she was in trouble, she always had turned to Toby. Even though telling him she was pregnant because of her own stupid decision to spend one night with the fast-talking, too-handsome-for-his-own-good Gio made her feel like an even bigger idiot.

Naomi still couldn't believe that one night of bad judgment and too much champagne had brought her to this. Toby was right, though. Even without Maverick shoving his nose into her business, she wouldn't have been able to hide her pregnancy for much longer. Loose tops and a strategically held handbag weren't going to disguise reality forever.

She shuddered a little in her seat. Naomi *hated* being pushed around by some nameless bully.

"You okay?" Toby asked, shooting her a quick look before turning his gaze back on the road in front of him.

"Not really," she admitted. "What the hell am I going to say to them?"

"The truth, Naomi," he said, reaching out to cover her hand with his. "Just tell them you're pregnant."

She held on to his hand and felt the warm, solid strength of him. "And when they ask who the father is?"

His mouth worked as if he wanted to say plenty but wasn't letting the words out. She appreciated the effort. He couldn't say anything about Gio that she hadn't been feeling anyway.

When she told Toby about the baby, he'd instantly proven to be a much better man than the one she'd slept with. Toby offered to help any way he could, which was just one of the things she loved most about him. He didn't judge. He was just *there*. Like the mountains. Or the ancient oaks surrounding his ranch house. He was sturdy. And dependable. And everything she'd never known in her life until him. Now she needed him more than ever.

The Prices lived in Pine Valley, an exclusive, gated golf course community where the mansions sat on huge lots behind tidy lawns where weeds didn't dare appear and "doing lunch" was considered a career. At least, that was how Naomi had always seen it. Growing up there hadn't been easy, again because her parents never seemed to know what to do with her. Maybe if she'd had a sibling to help her through, it might have been different. But alone, Naomi had always felt...unworthy, somehow.

Her thoughts came to an abrupt halt when Toby stopped at the gate. When he lowered the window to speak to the guard, a wave of early-summer heat invaded the truck cab.

"Who're you here to see?" the older man holding a clipboard asked.

Naomi knew that voice, so she leaned forward and smiled. "Hello, Stan. We're just coming in to see my parents."

"Naomi, it's good to see you." The man smiled, hit a button on the inside of his guard hut, and the high, wide gate instantly began to roll clear. "Your folks are at home. Bet they'll be happy to see you."

He waved them through, and she sat back. "Happy to see me? I don't think so."

Toby, still holding her hand, gave it a hard squeeze. She held on tightly, even when he would have released her. Because right now she needed his support—his friendship—more than ever.

The streets were beautiful, with big homes, most of them tucked behind shrubbery-lined fences. Even in a gated community, some of the very wealthy seemed to want their own personal security as well. Of course, not everyone's home was hidden away behind a wall of trees, hedges or stone. The palatial homes were all different, all custom designed and built. And the closer Toby's truck drew to the Price mansion, the more Naomi felt the swarms of butterflies soaring and diving in the pit of her stomach.

God, she couldn't remember a time when she'd felt at ease with her parents. It had always seemed as though she was putting on a production, playing the part of the perfect daughter. Only she never quite measured up. She wished things were different, but if wishes came true, she wouldn't be here in the first place, would she?

The driveway to her parents' house was long and curved, the better to display the banks of flowers tended with loving care by a squad of gardeners. The sweep of lawn was green and neatly trimmed, and trees were kept trained into balls on branches that looked as though they were trying to remember how to be real trees. The house itself was showy but tasteful, as her parents would accept nothing less— it was a blend of Cape Cod and Victorian. Pale gray with white trim and black shutters, it stood as grace-ful as a dancer in the center of the massive lot. The front door was white without a speck of dust to mar its surface. The windows gleamed in the sunlight and displayed curtains within, all drawn to exactly the same point.

It was like looking at a picture in an architec-tural magazine. Something staged, where no one really lived. And of course, she told herself silently, *no one did.* Instead of living, her parents existed on a stage where everyone knew their lines and no one ever strayed from the script. Well, except for Naomi.

Naomi herself had been the one time anything unexpected had happened in her parents' lives. She was, she knew, an "accident." A late-in-life baby who had caused them nothing but embarrassment at first, followed by years of disappointment. Her mother had been horrified to find herself pregnant at the age of forty-five and had endured the unwel-come pregnancy because to do otherwise would have been unthinkable for her. They raised her with care if not actual love and expected her not to make any further ripples in their life.

But Naomi had always caused ripples. Sometimes *waves*.

And today was going to be a tsunami.

"You're getting quiet," Toby said with a flicker of a smile. "Never a good sign."

She had to smile back. "Too much to think about."

She stared at the closed front door and dreaded

having to knock on it. Of course she would knock. And be announced by Matilda, the housekeeper who'd worked for her parents for twenty years. People didn't simply walk into her parents' house.

And her mind was going off on tangents because she didn't want to think about her real reason for being here.

"You've already made the hard decision," Toby pointed out. "You decided to keep the baby."

She had. Not that she cared at all about the baby's father, Naomi thought. But the baby was real to her. A person. *Her* child. How could she end the pregnancy? "I couldn't do anything else."

He reached out and took her hand for a quick squeeze. "I know. And I'll help however I can."

"I know you will," she said, holding on to his hand as she would a lifeline.

"You know," he said slowly, his deep voice rumbling through the truck cab, "there's no reason for you to be so worked up. You might want to consider that you're nearly thirty—"

"Hey!" She frowned at him. "I'm twenty-nine."

"My mistake," he said, mouth quirking, eyes shining. "But the point is, you've been on your own since college, Naomi. You don't have to explain your life to your parents."

"Easy for you to say," she countered. "Your mom and sister are your own personal cheering squad."

"True," he said, nodding. "But, Naomi, sooner or

later, you've got to take a stand and, instead of apologizing to your folks, just tell them what's what."

It sounded perfectly reasonable. And she knew he was right. But it didn't make the thought of actually doing it any easier to take. She dropped one hand to the slight mound of her belly and gave the child within a comforting pat. If there was ever a time to stand up to her parents, it was now. She was going to be a mother herself, for God's sake.

"You're right." She gave his hand another squeeze, then let go to release her seat belt. "I'm going to tell them about the baby and that the father isn't in the picture and I'll be a single mother and—" She stopped. "Oh, God."

He chuckled. "For a second there, you were raring to go."

"I still am," she insisted, in spite of, or maybe because of, the flurries of butterflies in her stomach. "Let's just go get it over with, okay?"

"And after, we'll hit the diner for lunch."

"Sounds like a plan," she said.

Two

Naomi took a deep breath in what she knew was a futile attempt to relax a little. There would be no relaxation until this meeting with her parents was over.

Toby came around the front of the truck, opened her door and waited for her to step down before asking, "You ready?"

"No. Yes. I don't know." Naomi shook her head, tugged at the hem of her cool green shirt as if she could somehow further disguise the still-tiny bump of her baby, then smoothed nervous hands along her hips. "Do I look all right?"

He tipped his head to one side, studied her, then smiled. "You look like you always do. Beautiful."

She laughed a little. Toby was really good for her self-esteem. Or, she thought, he would be, if she had any. God, what a pitiful thought. Of course she had self-esteem. It was just a bit like a roller-coaster ride. Sometimes up, sometimes down. Naomi'd be very happy if she could somehow reach a middle ground and stay there. But it was a constant battle between the two distinctly different voices in her head.

One telling her she was smart and talented and capable while the other whispered doubts. Amazing how much easier that dark voice was to believe.

And she was stalling.

"You're stalling," Toby said as if reading her mind. Her gaze snapped to his.

"Think you know me that well, do you?"

"Yeah," he said, a slow smile curving his mouth. "I do."

Okay, yes, he really did. Probably the only person she knew who could make that claim and mean it. Even her closest girlfriends, Cecelia and Simone, only knew about her what she wanted them to know. Naomi was really skilled at hiding her thoughts, at being who people expected or wanted her to be. But she never had to do that around Toby.

Taking her hand in his, he started for the front door. "Come on, Naomi. We'll talk to your folks, get this out in the open, then go have lunch so I can get a burger and you can nibble on a lettuce leaf."

She rolled her eyes behind his back, because damn it, he really *did* know her. All women watched their diets, didn't they? Especially *pregnant* women? At that thought, memories of that vile video Maverick had sent her rushed into her mind again. She saw the actress waddling, staggering across a mock-up of Naomi's own television set, and she shivered. She *refused* to waddle.

Naomi swallowed a groan and took the steps to the wide front porch beside Toby. He was still holding her hand, and she was grateful. A part of her brain shrieked at her that it was ridiculous for a grown woman to be so nervous about facing her parents. But that single voice was being systematically drowned out by a *choir* of other voices, reminding her that nothing good had ever come from having a chat with Franklin and Vanessa Price.

"You ready?"

She looked up into his eyes, shaded by his ever-present Stetson, and gathered the tattered threads of her courage. She had to be ready, because there was no other choice. "Yes."

"That'd be more believable if you weren't chewing on your bottom lip."

"Blast," she muttered and instinctively rubbed her lips together to smooth out her lipstick. "Fine. Now I'm ready."

"Damn right you are." He grinned, and her nerves settled. Really, Naomi wasn't sure what she'd ever done to deserve a best friend like Toby, but she was so thankful to have him.

Before she could talk herself out of it or worry on it any longer, she reached out and rapped her knuckles on the wide front door. Several seconds ticked past before it swung open to reveal Matilda, the Price family housekeeper and cook.

Tall, thin and dressed completely in black, Matilda wore her gunmetal-gray hair short and close to her head. Her complexion was pale and carved with wrinkles earned over a lifetime. She looked severe, humorless, although nothing could have been further from the truth. Matilda smiled in welcome.

"Miss Naomi," she said, stepping back to open the door wider. "You and Mr. Toby come in. I'll just tell your parents you're here. They're in the front parlor."

Of course they were, Naomi thought. She knew the Price family schedule and was aware that it never deviated. Late-morning tea began at eleven and ended precisely at eleven forty-five. After which her mother would drive into town to one of her charities and her father would go to the golf course or, on Tuesdays, the Texas Cattleman's Club to visit with his friends.

Waiting in the blessedly cool entry hall, Toby took his hat off, then bent to whisper, "Always makes me twitch when she calls me Mr. Toby."

"I know," Naomi said. "But propriety must be maintained at all times." Appearances, she knew, were very important to her parents. It had always mattered more how things looked than how things actually *were*.

She glanced around the home she'd grown up in. The interior hadn't changed much over the years.

Vanessa Price didn't care for change, and once she had things the way she wanted them, they stayed.

Cool, gray-veined white marble tile stretched from the entry all through the house. Paintings, in soothing pastel colors, hung in white frames on ecru walls, their muted hues the only splash of brightness in the decorating scheme. A Waterford crystal vase on the entry table held a huge bouquet of exotic flowers, all in varying shades of white, and the silence in the house was museum quality.

Idly, Naomi remembered being a child in this house and how she'd struggled to find her place. She never really did, which was why, she supposed, she still felt uncomfortable just being here.

Toby squeezed her hand as Matilda stepped into the hall and motioned for them to come ahead. Apparently, Naomi told herself, the king and queen were receiving today. The minute that thought entered her mind, she felt a quick stab of guilt. Her parents weren't evil people. They didn't deserve the mental barbs from their only child and wouldn't understand them if they knew how she really felt.

But at the same time, Naomi couldn't help wishing things were different. She wished, not for the first time, that she was able to just open the front door and sail in without being announced. She wished that her parents would be happy to see her. That she and her mom could curl up on the couch and talk about anything and everything. That her dad would sweep her up into a bear hug and call her "princess." That she wouldn't feel so tightly strung at the very thought of entering the formal parlor to face them.

But if wishes were real, she'd be sitting on a beach sipping a margarita right now.

Her parents were seated in matching Victorian chairs, with a tea table directly in front of them. The rest of the room was just as fussily decorated, looking like a curator's display of Louis XIV furniture. Nothing in the house invited people to settle in or, God forbid, put their feet on a table.

The windows allowed a wide swath of sunlight to spear into the room, illuminating the beige- and eggshell-colored furniture, the gold leaf edging the desk on the far wall, the white shades on crystal lamps and the complete lack of welcome in her parents' eyes. It was eleven thirty. They still had fifteen minutes of teatime left, and Naomi had just ruined it.

She was about to ruin a lot more.

"Hello, Mom, Dad." She smiled, steeled herself and released Toby's hand to cross the room. She bent down to kiss the cheek her mother offered, and then when her father stood up to greet Toby, she kissed her dad's cheek, too.

"Hello, dear," Vanessa Price said. "This is a surprise. Toby, it's nice to see you. Would you like to join us for tea? I can have Matilda brew fresh."

"No, ma'am, thank you," Toby said after shaking Franklin's hand and stepping back to range himself at Naomi's side.

Franklin Price was a handsome man in his seventies. He wore a perfectly tailored suit and his silver hair was swept back from a high, wide forehead. His blue eyes were sharp but curious as they landed on his daughter. Vanessa was petite, and though in her seventies, she presented, as always, a perfect picture. Her startlingly white hair was trimmed into a modern but flattering cut, and her figure was trim, since she had spent most of her life dieting to ensure it. Her jewel-bright blue summer dress looked casually elegant and at the same time served to make Naomi feel like a hag.

"Is there something wrong, dear?" Vanessa set her Limoges china teacup down onto the table and then folded her hands neatly in her lap.

There was her opening, Naomi thought, and braced herself to jump right in.

"Actually, yes, there is," she admitted, and glanced at her father to see his concerned frown. "You've both heard about this Maverick who's been contacting people in Royal for the last several months?"

"Distasteful," Vanessa said primly with a mild shake of her head.

"I'll agree with your mother. Whoever it is needs to be apprehended and charged," her father said. "Prying into people's private lives is despicable."

"He's caused a lot of trouble," Toby said and took Naomi's hand to give it a squeeze.

Her mother caught the gesture, and her eyes narrowed in suspicion.

"Maverick contacted *me* this morning," Naomi

blurted out before she could lose her dwindling nerve entirely.

"You?" Vanessa lifted one hand to the base of her throat, her fingers sliding through a string of pearls. "Whatever could he do to you?"

Still frowning, Franklin Price looked from Naomi to Toby and back again. "What is it, girl?"

Oh, here it comes, she told herself. And once the words were said, everything would change forever. There was no choice. Toby was right—she couldn't keep hiding her baby bump with loose clothing. There would come a time when the truth just wouldn't remain hidden.

"I'm pregnant," she said flatly, "and Maverick is about to send a video out onto the internet telling everyone."

"Pregnant?" Vanessa slumped back against her chair, and now her hand tightened at the base of her throat as if she were trying to massage air into her lungs.

"Who's the father?" Franklin's demand was quiet but no less fierce.

"Oh, Naomi," her mother said on a defeated sigh. "How could you let this happen?"

"Who did this to you?" her father asked again.

As if she'd been held down against her will, Naomi thought on an internal groan. Oh, she couldn't tell them about Gio. About how stupid she'd been. How careless. How could she say that the baby's father was an Italian gigolo with whom she'd spent a single night? But what else *could* she say?

They were waiting expectantly, her mother just a little horrified, her father leaning more toward cold anger. She'd proven a disappointment. Again. And it was only going to get worse.

"I'm the father," Toby said when she opened her mouth to speak.

"What?" she whispered, horrified.

Toby gave her a quick smile, then fixed his gaze on her father. "That's why I came here with Naomi today. We wanted to tell you together that we're having a baby and we're going to be married."

Naomi could only stare at him in stunned silence. She hadn't expected him to do this. And she didn't know what to do about it now. A ribbon of relief shot whiplike through her, and even as it did, Naomi knew she couldn't let him do this. As much as she appreciated the chivalry, this was her mess and she'd find a way to—

"We wanted to tell you before anyone else," Toby went on smoothly. "Naomi's going to be living with me at my ranch."

"Toby—"

He didn't even glance at her. "No point in her staying at her condo in town, so she's moving to Paradise Ranch in a few days."

"But—" She tried to speak again. To correct him. To argue. To say *something*, but her mother spoke up, effectively keeping Naomi quiet.

"Living together isn't something I would usually approve," she said primly, "but as you're engaged, I think propriety has been taken care of."

Propriety. Naomi had often thought her mother would have been happier living in the Regency period. Where manners were all and society followed strict rules.

"Engaged." Her mother said the word again, as if savoring it. "Oh, Naomi, you're marrying Toby McKittrick. It's just wonderful."

Vanessa rose quickly, moved to stand beside her husband and then actually beamed her pleasure.

Naomi had never been on the receiving end of that smile before, so it threw her a little. Then she realized exactly what her mother had said. She wasn't thrilled about the baby, but about her daughter marrying Toby. Handsome. Stable. *Wealthy* Toby McKittrick. That was the kind of announcement Vanessa Price could get behind.

And that realization only made Naomi furious. At Toby. She hadn't expected her parents to be supportive, but having Toby ride to the rescue felt, after that first burst of relief, more than a little annoying. She'd only wanted him here for moral support. Not to sweep in and lie to save her. The whole purpose of coming here to tell her parents the truth was to get it over with.

Now not only had the moment of truth been postponed, but Toby had added to the mess with a lie she'd eventually have to answer for.

"Toby—"

He looked down at her, gave her a smile, then surprised her into being quiet with a quick, hard kiss that left her lips buzzing. Shock rattled her. He'd never kissed her before, and though it hadn't been a lover's kiss, it wasn't exactly a brotherly kiss, either.

When he was sure she was shocked speechless, he turned to face her parents. "Naomi's a little upset. She wanted to be the one to tell you about us getting married, but I just couldn't help myself. And we're heading over to her place today to start packing for the move, so we wanted to see you first."

"Understandable," Franklin said with an approving nod at Toby, followed by a worried glance at Naomi. "I'll say, you worried me there for a moment with news of a pregnancy. But since you're marrying, I'm sure it's fine."

Great. All it had taken to win her parents' approval was the right marriage. God. Maybe they *were* in the Regency period.

"I don't see your ring," Vanessa pointed out with a deliberate look at Naomi's left hand.

Naomi sighed, then lifted her gaze to Toby as if to demand, *this was your idea—fix it.*

Then he did. His way.

"We're going right into town to see about that. And if I can't find what I want there," Toby announced, "we'll drive into Houston." He dropped one arm around Naomi's shoulders and pulled her up close to him. "But we wanted you to know our news before you heard about Maverick's video."

"No one pays attention to people of that sort," Vanessa said with assuredness.

Naomi wondered how she could say it, since the whole town of Royal had been talking about nothing else *but* Maverick for months. But Vanessa didn't care to see what she considered ugliness, and it was amazingly easy for her to close her eyes to anything that might disrupt her orderly world.

"Now, Naomi, don't you worry over this Maverick person," her mother said firmly. "You and Toby have done nothing wrong. Perhaps you haven't done things in the proper *order*—"

Meaning, Naomi thought, courtship, engagement, marriage and *then* a baby. Still, her mother was willing to overlook all that for the happy news that her daughter would finally be *settled*, with a more than socially acceptable husband. Which meant that when she had to tell them that she absolutely was *not* going to marry Toby, the fallout would be epic.

"We should be going now. We need to get Naomi all moved in and settled at the ranch. Sorry for interrupting your tea," Toby was saying, and Naomi told herself to snap out of her thoughts.

He was going to hurry her out of the house before she could tell her parents the truth. And she was going to let him. Sure, she'd have to confess eventually, but right this minute? Naomi just wanted to be far, far away.

"Nonsense," Franklin said. "You're always welcome here, Toby. Especially now."

Naomi muffled a sigh. All it had taken was the promise of a "good" marriage to fling the Price family doors wide-open. She could only imagine how fast they would slam shut once they knew the truth.

"I appreciate that, Mr. Price."

"Franklin, boy. You call me Franklin."

"Yes, sir, I will," Toby promised, but didn't. "Now if you'll excuse us, I think we'll just go get Naomi's things and find that ring we talked about before Naomi changes her mind and leaves me heartbroken."

Vanessa's eyes widened. "Oh, she wouldn't!"

Toby winked at Naomi, completely ignoring how tense she'd gone beside him. To her parents, this suddenly imagined marriage was very real. She knew Toby thought he'd made things better, but in reality, he'd only made the whole situation more…complicated.

"You two enjoy yourselves, and, Naomi, we'll talk about a lovely wedding real soon," her mother called after her. "We'll want to have the ceremony before you start…*showing*."

"Oh, God," Naomi whispered.

Toby squeezed her hand and hurried her out of the house. Once outside, he bundled her into his truck before she could say anything, so it wasn't until he was in the truck himself, firing the engine, that Naomi was able to demand, "What were you thinking?"

He blew out a breath, squinted into the sun and steered the truck away from the front door and back down the flower-lined drive. "I was thinking that I didn't like the way your folks were looking at you."

His profile was stern, his mouth tight and a muscle in his jaw flexing, telling her he was grinding his teeth together. Naomi sighed a little. She hadn't thought he'd take her parents' reaction so personally on her behalf, though in retrospect, she should have. He'd always been the kind of man to stand up for someone being bullied. He took the side of the underdog because that was just who Toby was. But she didn't want to be one of his mercy rescues.

"I appreciate the misguided chivalry," she said, striving for patience. "But it just makes everything harder, Toby. Now I'm going to have to tell them that I'm not moving in with you, our engagement is off and make up some reason for it—which my mother will never accept—and then I'll still be a single mother and they'll be even more disappointed in me than ever."

"They don't have to be." He shot her one fast look. "We move you out to Paradise today. We get married. Just like I said."

Naomi just stared at him. Since he was driving, he didn't take his eyes off the road again, so she couldn't see if he was joking or not. But he *had* to be joking. "You're not serious."

"Dead serious."

"Toby," she argued, "that's nuts. I mean, it was a sweet thing to do—"

"Screw *sweet*," he snapped with a shake of his head. "I wasn't doing it to be sweet and, okay, fine, I didn't really think about it before saying it, but once the words were out, they made sense."

"In a crazy, upside-down world, maybe. Here? Not so much."

"Think about it, Naomi."

She lifted one hand to rub her forehead, hoping to ease the throbbing headache centered there. "Haven't been able to do much else since you blurted out all that."

"Then think about *this*. There's no point in you raising a baby on your own when I'm standing right here."

"It's not your baby," she pointed out.

"It could be," he countered just as quickly. "I'd be a good father. A good husband."

"That's not the point."

"Then what *is*?"

She lifted both hands and tugged hard on her own hair. Nope, she wasn't dreaming any of this, which meant she had to get through to him. What he'd just said had touched her. Deeply. To know that he was willing to throw himself on a metaphorical grenade for her meant more than she could say. But that didn't mean she would actually allow him to claim another man's child as his own. It wouldn't be fair to him.

"There are many, many points to be made, but the main one is, I'm not your responsibility," she said, keeping her voice calm and firm.

"Never said you were," he said. "You are my friend, though."

"Best friend," she corrected, still looking at his profile. "Absolutely."

"Then accept that as your friend I want to help you."

"Toby, I can't let you do that."

"You're not *letting* me, I'm just doing it." He stopped at a four-way intersection and, when it was clear, drove on toward Royal. "It makes sense, Naomi. For all of us, the baby included. You really want to be all alone in that snazzy condo in Royal? Or would you rather be with me out at the ranch? If we're living together, that baby has two parents to look out for it. And, big plus, you can stop tying yourself into knots over your folks."

"So you're trying to save me." Just as she'd suspected. "This is all some grand gesture for my sake."

"And my own," he said, then muttered something under his breath and pulled the truck over to the side of the road. He parked, turned off the engine, then shifted in his seat to face her.

His eyes, the clear, cool aqua of a tropical sea, fixed on her, and Naomi read steely determination in that stare. She'd seen him this way before. Whenever he had an idea for one of his inventions, he got that *I will not be stopped* look on his face, in his eyes. If someone told him no about something, he took it as a personal challenge. Once Toby decided on a course of action, it was nearly impossible to get him to change his mind. This time, she told herself, it had to be different.

"I'm not a saint, and I'm not trying to rescue you."

"Could have fooled me," she murmured.

He sighed heavily, turned his gaze out on the road stretched out in front of them for a long second or two, then looked back at her. "Hell, Naomi, we're best friends. We're both single, and we can raise the baby together. Helping each other. This could work, if you'll let it."

A part of her, she was ashamed to admit, wanted to say yes and accept the offer he shouldn't be making. But he was her friend, so she couldn't take advantage of him like that. "I don't need a husband, Toby. I can raise my child on my own."

Now he sent her a cool, hard stare. "You forget, my mother was a single mom after my dad died. I watched how hard it was for her to be mother and father to me and my sister. To work and take care of the house. To run around after me and Scarlett with no one to help out. You really think I want to sit by and watch you go through the same damn thing?"

She bit her lip. She had forgotten about Toby's family. His mother, Joyce, was a smart, capable, lovely woman who had worked hard to raise her kids on her own. Now Toby was not just a successful rancher, but a wealthy inventor, and his younger sister, Scarlett, was a veterinarian. "Your mother did a great job with both of you."

His features evened out, and he gave her a smile. "And we thank you. But my point is, you don't have to do it the hard way like my mom did. Mom didn't have anyone to help her. You have me."

"I know," she said, taking a breath to calm the anger bubbling inside. "I really do know. But you don't have to marry me, Toby."

"Who said anything about *have* to?" he asked. "I want to. We're good together, Naomi. There's plenty of room at the ranch. You can take over one of the bedrooms for an office. It's not far from the studio where you film your show…"

True. All true. There was a small studio at the edge of Royal where her cable TV show, *Fashion Sense*, was recorded once a week. And to be honest, being at the ranch would get her away from most of the gossiping tongues in town, and once Maverick's video hit, she'd be grateful for that.

"It's a great idea, Naomi. Hell, even your parents liked it."

She choked out a laugh. "Of course they did. Toby McKittrick—inventor, rancher, wealthy. I'm surprised my mother didn't squeal."

He gave her a half smile and a slow shake of his head. "You're being too hard on her. On both of them."

"I know that, too," she said with a sigh. She smoothed her fingertips over her knees. "They're not evil people. They're not even really mean. They just live in a very narrow world and it's never had room for me."

He reached out and took her hand, stilling nervous fingers. "There's room for you with me."

"Toby..." Naomi didn't know what to think. Or feel. He was right in that they were good together. They were already friends, and maybe a marriage of convenience would be good for both of them. But was it fair to him? "If we're married, you can't find someone for real."

"Not interested," he said firmly with a shake of his head. "Been there already, and it didn't end well."

Naomi sighed again. She couldn't blame him for feeling burned in the love department. She could, however, blame the woman who'd hurt him enough that Toby had built a wall around his heart that was so tall and thick it had taken Naomi months to reach past it.

"Fine. You're not looking for love. Neither am I," she added in a mutter. "But that doesn't mean..."

"Think about it."

"But no one will believe it."

"Your parents did."

She waved that aside. "That's because they don't know me. My friends—"

"Are so wrapped up in their own happily-ever-afters they won't question it."

"Your family—"

He scowled thoughtfully, but a moment later, his

expression cleared. Those amazing eyes fixed on her, he said, "Okay, I'll tell my family the truth. Don't want to lie to them anyway. Does that work for you?"

"They won't like it," she said, and silently added, *they'll blame me*.

"Mom and Scarlett both like you already, so what's the problem?"

"I don't know if I want to be married," she said simply. "You're my best friend, Toby. It'll be... *weird*."

He laughed and shook his head. "Doesn't have to be. Think of it as a marriage of convenience. We're together because of the baby. No sex. Just friends who live together."

No sex. Well, it wasn't as if she was a wildly sexual person anyway. In fact, until that single night with Gio, she hadn't been with anyone in more than a year. And since Gio, she'd avoided *all* men except for Toby. So going without sex wouldn't be that terrible, would it? Oh, God.

"I'm not saying we become monks," Toby pointed out as though he could read her thoughts. "If one of us meets someone, we'll work that out then. In the meantime, we're together."

Toby watched her and wondered what the hell she was arguing about. Anyone could see this was a good idea. Though he could admit that he hadn't come up with it until that moment when Vanessa Price gave her daughter the cool look of disappointment at news of the baby. Damned if he could just stand there while Naomi tried to explain about the baby's father and how he was a worthless player. So, before he'd really considered it, he'd blurted out the lie. And it had felt…right.

Why not get married to his best friend? Whether she knew it or not, she was going to need help with the baby. And as long as they kept things between them platonic, everything would work out fine. Yeah, he was attracted to her. What man wouldn't be? But he wasn't going to act on that attraction, so a marriage of convenience was the best solution here.

"Well?" he asked, gaze fixed on hers. "What do you think?"

"I think you're crazy," she said on a half laugh.

"That's been said before," he reminded her. "People have been talking about crazy Toby and his weird inventions for years."

Nervously, she pushed her hair back from her face, and the early-afternoon sunlight caught a few threads of copper, making them gleam. "If we do this, we'll both be crazy."

"Worse things to be, Naomi."

She smiled. "Are you sure about this?"

He tipped his head to one side and gave her a look. "When have you ever known me to say something without meaning every damn word?"

"Never," she said, nodding. "It's one of the things I like best about you. I always know what you're thinking, because you don't play games."

"Games are for kids, Naomi. Neither one of us is a kid."

"No, we're not." She met his gaze squarely and took a deep breath. "I'm a city girl. What'll I do on a ranch?"

"Whatever needs doing," he said.

She laughed shortly. "We really must be crazy. Okay. I'll marry you and not have sex with you."

He grinned and winked. "Now, how many people can say that?" Turning in his seat, he fired up the truck, put it in gear and steered out onto the road again, headed for town. "We'll go get lunch, and then we'll go ring shopping."

"No."

"No?" He glanced at her, surprised.

"No ring," she said, shaking her head. "We don't need an engagement ring, Toby, and I don't want you buying one for me when it wouldn't really mean what it should. You know?"

He understood and couldn't say he disagreed. Their marriage would be a joining of friends, not some celebration of love, after all. "What's your mama going to say?"

Smiling sadly, Naomi said, "Even if we'd gotten one, she'd have found something wrong with it anyway."

They slipped into silence. Toby took her hand for the rest of the drive but left her to her thoughts.

Three

Toby opened the door to the Royal Diner, steered Naomi inside and stopped. Every person in the place turned to look at them, and he knew. Maverick had done as promised. That stupid video was on the internet, and it seemed clear that it was the hot topic in Royal.

The welcoming scents of coffee, French fries and burgers greeted them. Classic rock played on the old-fashioned jukebox in the corner, and noise from the kitchen drifted out of the pass-through, but other than that, the silence was telling.

"Let's go," Naomi said, and tugged at his hand.

"Not a chance," Toby countered. Then, bending his head down to hers, he whispered, "Do you really want them to think you're scared?"

He knew it was just the right note to take when she squared her shoulders, lifted her chin and stood there like a queen before peasants. Toby hid a smile, because in just a second or two the woman he knew so well had reemerged, squashing the part of her that wanted to run and hide.

A couple of seconds ticked past and then the diner customers returned to their meals, though most of them looked to be having hushed conversations. It didn't take a genius to guess what they were talking about.

He gave Naomi's hand a squeeze, then took off his hat and smiled at Amanda Battle as she hurried over. Married to Sheriff Nathan Battle, who was doing everything he could to find out who this Maverick person was, Amanda owned the diner, along with her sister, Pam.

"Well, hi, you two," she said with a deliberately bright smile. "Booth or table?"

"Booth if you've got it," Toby said quickly, knowing Naomi wouldn't want to be seated in the middle of the room. Hell, he still half expected her to make a break for the door.

"Right. Down there along the window's good." Amanda gave Naomi a pat on the shoulder and said, "I'll get you some water and menus."

They walked past groups of friends and neighbors, nodding as they went, and Toby felt Naomi stiffening alongside him. She was maintaining, but it was costing her. She wasn't happy, and he couldn't blame her. Hell, he hated this whole mess for her.

The familiarity of the diner did nothing to ease the tension in Naomi's shoulders. The Royal Diner hadn't changed much over the years. Oh, it had all been updated, but Amanda and Pam had kept the basics the same, just freshening it all up. The floor was still black-and-white squares, the booths and counter stools were still bright red vinyl, and chrome was the accent of choice. The white walls held pictures of Royal through the years, and it was still the place to go if you wanted the best burger anywhere.

Once they were seated, Amanda came back quickly, set water glasses in front of them and handed out menus. Smiling down at them, she said, "I guess congratulations are in order."

"Oh, God," Naomi murmured, and her shoulders slumped, as if all the air had been let out of her body. "You've seen the video."

Amanda gave her a friendly pat and said, "I'm not talking about the video, honey. Don't worry about that. That nosy bastard has been poking into too many lives, so everyone here knows they could be next. Looks like this Maverick is moving around pretty quick, so he'll be onto someone new before you know it and you'll be old news."

Toby could have kissed her. "She's right."

Naomi looked at him, and he read resignation and worry in her eyes. "Doesn't help much, though. The whole town knows I'm pregnant now."

"Naomi, most of us guessed anyway," Amanda said. At Naomi's stunned expression, Amanda added, "You've never worn loose shirts and long cover-ups in your life."

Toby grinned. "She's got a point."

Naomi blew out a breath and gave him a rueful smile. "So much for my brilliant disguises."

"Oh—" Amanda waved one hand "—it probably fooled the men." She gave Toby an amused glance. "You guys don't really notice much. But women know a baby bump when they see one being hidden."

Naomi nodded. "Right."

"But I wasn't congratulating you on the baby anyway," Amanda continued. "Though sure, best wishes. I was talking about your engagement to Toby here."

Now it was his turn to be stunned. "How did you find out about that already?"

"Remember where we live, honey," Amanda said with a shake of her head that sent her dark blond ponytail swinging behind her. "Naomi's mother called one of her friends, who called somebody else, who called Pam's sister-in-law, who called Pam, who told me."

Naomi just blinked at her. Toby felt the same way. He had always known that gossip flew in Royal as fast as the tornadoes that occasionally swept across Texas. But this had to be a record.

"We just left my parents' house twenty minutes ago," Naomi complained.

"What's your point?" Amanda asked, grinning.

Helplessly shaking her head, Naomi said, "I guess I don't have one."

"There you go," Amanda said. "And so you know, most everybody's talking more about the engagement than that video. I mean, really." She laughed a little. "Maverick thought he was being funny, I guess, but him mocking you like that? Didn't make sense. People in Royal know Naomi Price has got style. So making that woman look so big and sloppy just didn't have the smack he probably thought it would."

Toby saw how those words hit Naomi, and once again, he could have kissed Amanda for saying just the right thing. She was right, of course. Naomi, even with her pregnancy showing, would be just as stylish as ever. That video was meant to hurt her, humiliate her, but he knew Naomi well enough to know that after the initial embarrassment passed, she'd rise above it and come out the winner.

"But you two engaged," Amanda said with a wink. "Now, that's news worth chewing on."

"I hate being gossiped about," Naomi muttered.

"In a small town," Amanda pointed out, "we all take our turn at the top of the rumor mill eventually."

"Doesn't make it any easier," she said.

"Suppose not, but at least people are pleased for you," Amanda said.

"Well, it's good the news is out." Toby spoke up, getting both women's attention. "And to celebrate our engagement, I'll have the cowboy burger with fries and some sweet tea."

"Got it. Naomi?"

"Small salad, please," she said. "Dressing on the side. And unsweetened tea."

"That's no way to feed a baby," Amanda muttered, but nodded. "And not even close to a celebration, but okay. Be out in a few minutes."

When she was gone, Toby took a drink of water, set the glass down and said, "She's right. That baby needs more than dry lettuce."

"Don't start," she warned, and turned her gaze on the street beyond the window. "I'm not going to end up waddling through the last of this pregnancy, Toby."

Irritation spiked, but he swallowed it back. Naomi had been on a damn diet the whole time he'd known her. In fact, he could count on the fingers of one hand how many times he'd seen her actually *enjoy* eating. She was so determined to stave off any reminders of the chubby little girl she'd once been, she counted every calorie as if it meant her life.

But it wasn't just her now. That baby was going to need protein. And once she was living with him on the ranch, he'd make sure she ate more than a damn rabbit did. But that battle was for later. Not today.

"Fine."

"I can't believe people already know about the engagement," Naomi said, looking back at him. Reaching out, she grabbed her paper napkin and began tearing at the edges with nervous fingers.

"At least they're talking about us, not the video,"

Toby pointed out and took another sip of water. His gaze was fixed on hers, and he didn't like that haunted look that still colored her eyes.

Scowling, she muttered, "I don't want them talking about me at all."

Toby laughed, and laughed even harder when she glared at him.

"What's so funny?" she demanded.

Scrubbing one hand across his face, he did his best to wipe away the amusement still tickling him. Keeping his voice low, he said, "You, honey. You *love* being talked about. Always have."

When she would have argued, he shook his head and leaned across the table toward her. "You were homecoming queen and a cheerleader—at college you were the president of your sorority. Now? You still love it. Why else would you have your own TV show? You like being the center of attention, Naomi, and why shouldn't you?"

"I didn't do all that just to be talked about," she argued.

"I know that," he said and slid one hand across the table to cover hers. "You did all of it because you liked it. Because you wanted to." *And because it was the attention you never got at home and that fed something in you that's still hungry today.*

"I did. And I like doing my show, knowing people watch and talk about it." She leaned toward him, too, even as she pulled her hand from beneath his. "But there's a difference, Toby, between people talking about my work and talking about my life."

"Not by much, there isn't," he said and leaned back, laying one arm along the top of the booth bench. "Naomi, we live in a tiny town in Texas. People talk. Always have. Always will. What matters is how you deal with it."

"I'm dealing," she grumbled, and he wanted to smile again but was half-worried she might kick him under the table if he did.

"No, you're not." He tipped his head to one side and gave her a look that said *be honest*. "You're nearly five months along with that baby, and you just now told your folks."

"That's different." Her fingers tore at the napkin again until she had quite the pile of confetti going.

"And when we walked in here and people turned to look, you would have walked right back out if I hadn't gotten in your way."

She frowned at him, and the flash in her eyes told him he was lucky she hadn't kicked him. "I don't like it when you're a know-it-all."

"Sure you do." She lifted one eyebrow again, and he had to admire it. Never had been able to do it himself. "Look, either you can let this Maverick win, by curling up and hiding out…or you can hold your head up like the tough woman I know you are and not let some mystery creep dictate how your life goes."

"Using logic isn't fair."

"Yeah, I know."

She sat back in the booth and continued to fiddle with the paper napkin in front of her. It was nearly gone now, and he told himself to remember to ask Amanda for more.

"Toby, I don't want to let Maverick win. To run my decisions. But isn't that what I'm doing by agreeing to marry you?"

"No." He straightened up now, leaned toward her and met her gaze dead-on. "If you were doing what he wanted, you'd be locked in a closet crying somewhere. Do you think that bastard wants you to be with me and happy? Do you think he wants you turning the whole town on its ear so they don't even think about his stupid video?"

"No, I suppose not," she murmured.

"Damn straight." He laid his hand over hers again and quieted those nervous fingers. "You're taking charge, Naomi."

"That's not how it feels."

"I can see that. But trust me on this—you're the one calling the shots here. You've left Maverick in your dust already, and he's only going to get dustier from here on out." He squeezed her fingers until he felt her squeeze back. "Us getting married? That's a good thing. For all of us, baby included."

She sighed. "I just don't know how this day got away from me. One minute I'm dreading talking to my parents, and the next I'm engaged to *you*."

"I don't know why you think marriage to me is such a damn hardship."

Her gaze narrowed on his. "I didn't say that—fine," she said when he smiled. "Make jokes. We'll see how funny you think it is when I'm living at the ranch with you."

He shrugged to show her he wasn't bothered. "You're a good cook and you're already pregnant, so all I need to do is keep you barefoot and in the kitchen."

She laughed then slapped one hand to her mouth to hold the rest of it inside. Toby grinned at her. God, he loved hearing that wild, deep laughter come out of such a wisp of a woman.

"You're making me laugh so I won't obsess about what a mess my life is."

"Is it working?"

Thinking about it for a second or two, she finally said, "Yes. So, thanks."

"You're welcome."

He watched her as, still smiling to herself, she looked out the window at the little town still buzzing over their news. Royal had seen a lot of upheaval over the last few months. Thanks to the mysterious Maverick, things had been changing right and left. It wasn't just him and Naomi making a major shift in their lives. Some of Toby's friends had made sudden changes that at the time had completely surprised Toby.

Hell, there was Wes Jackson for one. Toby never would have thought that man would settle down and get married, and now the man had a wife, a daughter and another baby on the way. Tom and Emily Knox had worked out their problems and seemed stronger than ever, and even Naomi's best friends, Cecelia and Simone, were happy and settled into real relationships.

Toby knew that Maverick had been at the heart of all those changes. Sure, the man had been trying to ruin people, but in a roundabout way he'd helped them instead.

Toby had stood on the sidelines, watching his friends take steps forward in their lives, and wondered when he would be Maverick's target. But the nameless bastard hadn't come for him at all, but Naomi. Seeing her worried, upset, had torn at him enough that he was willing to put aside his anti-marriage stance. And actually, the more he thought about it, the more marrying Naomi made sense. He'd get a family out of it without having to worry about getting in too deep emotionally.

All he had to do was make sure she didn't back out.

"Hey, Toby," Clay Everett called out, "you got a minute?"

"Sure." Toby glanced at Naomi. "I'll be right back."

She nodded when he slid out of the booth and walked to the table where Clay and Shane Delgado were having lunch. Toby's strides were long and easy, as if he had all the time in the world. He was tall and confident and seemed so damn sure that they were doing the right thing, and Naomi really wished she shared that certainty.

Clay, Shane and Toby were all ranchers, so no doubt they were talking about horses or grazing pastures or summer water levels. Her gaze swept them all quickly. Shane had long brown hair, a perpetual five o'clock shadow and a killer smile. He was both a rancher and a real estate developer. Clay was the strong, silent type with short brown hair, a lot of muscles and a limp he'd earned riding the rodeo circuit. After the accident that had ended his rodeo career, Clay had started a cloud computing company and had found even more success. Then there was Toby. Toby was both an inventor and a rancher and, from Naomi's point of view, the most gorgeous of them all.

She blinked at that thought and realized that for the first time she was looking at Toby without the filter of the best friend thing. And it was an eye-opener. When he looked up at her and gave her a slow smile, something inside her lit up—so Naomi instantly shut it down.

Surprise at her own reaction to him had her tearing her gaze from his and reminding herself that this marriage was a platonic one and now was *not* the time to start noting things she never had before. Toby was standing for her like no one else ever had. He was being the friend he always had been, and she should be grateful. Maybe, eventually, she would be.

But at the moment, her own pride was nicked, and Naomi hated knowing that she needed the help. He was right, of course. Raising a baby on her own was a daunting idea, but she would have done it. Now she didn't have to face the future alone. She had her best friend standing beside her. The only real question was, was it fair to *him*?

"Here's your tea," Amanda said, sliding two tall glasses of icy amber liquid onto the table.

"Oh, thanks." Naomi reached for her glass and took a sip.

"It's decaf tea for you, sweetie." Amanda tossed a glance at Toby, Clay and Shane, deep into a conversation, then looked back at Naomi. "I'd expect to see a smile on your face, just getting engaged and all."

Naomi sighed a little. Amanda Battle was a few years older than her, but growing up in the same small town meant they'd known each other forever. Amanda's blond hair was pulled back into a ponytail, and her eyes were sharp and thoughtful as she studied Naomi. "What's going on, Naomi? A woman engaged to a man like Toby McKittrick should be all smiles—and you're not."

"It just happened so fast," Naomi said, already leaning into the lie she and Toby had created out of thin air.

"Not too fast, since you're carrying his baby," Amanda reminded her.

"True." Toby had claimed the baby as his already, so that didn't even feel like a lie. Especially since the baby's actual father didn't even know about the pregnancy. "But he sort of sprung the proposal on me just this morning and I haven't gotten used to it yet, I guess." The best lies had a touch of truth in them, right?

"I know it must feel like a lot," Amanda said, laying one hand on Naomi's shoulder in sympathy. "But I was in your shoes once, remember?"

She did remember, and because she did, Naomi couldn't understand why Amanda was being so nice to her. Several years ago, Amanda had been pregnant and agreed to marry Nathan Battle for the sake of the baby. But then she miscarried and called the wedding off. Amanda had left town after that but had come back a few years later when her father died, and almost instantly, she and Nathan had reconnected and set the gossip train humming. Today, though, Nathan and Amanda had two kids and were so happily married there were practically hearts and flowers circling Amanda's head.

But back then, Naomi and her friends Cecelia and Simone were at the height of their mean girl reputations, and though it shamed her to admit it, Naomi had spread every ounce of gossip about Amanda that had come her way. Shaking her head at the crowd of memories that made her want to cringe, she managed to ask, "Why are you being so nice to me?"

Amanda threw another glance at Toby to make sure he wasn't on his way back, then she slid onto the bench seat opposite Naomi. Tipping her head to one side, Amanda studied her for a second, then said, "Because I've been the center of gossip and I know how ugly it can make you feel. And, Naomi, you're not who you were back then."

"How can you be sure?"

"Because the old Naomi wouldn't be feeling bad about any of it."

Yes, she would have, Naomi thought. Even back then, when she'd been the queen bee, guilt had haunted her whenever she allowed herself to think about what she'd said or done. Now Naomi released a pent-up breath she hadn't even realized she'd been holding. All the years she'd been coming to the Royal Diner, she'd never really had an actual conversation with Amanda. Years ago, it was because they were too far apart in age, and Naomi was too busy mocking people to make herself feel better. And then later, she'd been too ashamed of her past actions to talk to her. A small smile curved Naomi's mouth. "Thanks for that."

Amanda smiled again, shot a quick glance at the kitchen pass-through, then looked at Naomi. "Most of us did things when we were young and stupid that we come to regret." Her smile turned rueful, but her green eyes never left Naomi's. "So if you're lucky enough to grow out of the stupid, then you have a second chance to be who you want to be."

"You make it sound easy."

"It's not," the other woman said. "But you already know that. You started that fashion show—which, by the way, I never miss—and you're building a future with Toby."

"True." But if you were planning that future on a lie, did it count? Could it work? Not questions she could ask out loud. "Thanks. For the pep talk and, well, everything."

"No problem." Amanda scooted out of the booth, stood up and patted Naomi's shoulder again. "Toby's a good guy. You should celebrate."

Nodding, Naomi watched Toby laughing with his friends. Texas cowboys, all three of them. And handsome enough to have women lining up just to take a look at them. Her heart twisted as her gaze landed on Toby just as he lifted his head, caught her eye and winked. That flicker of something bright and hot sparkled inside her again, and though she fought to ignore it, the heat lingered.

In reflex, Naomi returned that smile and quietly hoped that this marriage didn't cost her her best friend.

Toby knew he'd catch his mom and sister off guard with his announcement. After lunch, where he'd finally convinced Naomi to take a small bite of his burger, Toby dropped her off at her condo to start packing. Then he'd driven straight to Oak Ridge Farms, his family ranch.

It was smaller than his own spread, but the ties binding him to the land ran strong and deep. His mother rented out most of the acreage to other ranchers and farmers, and his sister had her veterinary clinic in the remodeled barn. But no matter what changes took place, it would always be the McKittrick Ranch, and steering his truck up the drive would always make him feel the tug of memories.

He knew that he would beat the news of his engagement home, because it didn't matter how fast word was spreading throughout Royal. His mother, Joyce McKittrick, didn't approve of gossip, so she'd been cut out of the rumor loop years ago. As for his sister, Scarlett was too busy caring for the local animals to waste time or interest on gossip.

Toby had told Naomi that he wouldn't lie to his family. So after he explained the whole situation to his mom and sister, he waited for the reaction. He'd expected they'd be surprised. He hadn't expected them to be so happy about it. Especially since he'd made it clear that love didn't have a thing to do with his reasons for this marriage.

"You're marrying Naomi?" Scarlett McKittrick squealed a little, then leaped up from her chair at the kitchen table and ran around to hug her brother. "It's about time."

"What?" Toby looked at his younger sister when she pulled back to grin at him.

"Well, come on," Scarlett said. "You two have been tight for years, and even a blind person would have seen the sparks between you."

Sparks? There were sparks? Toby frowned a little as he realized that maybe all the lustful thoughts he'd been entertaining for so long had been obvious. Well, that was lowering, if his sister noticed something that he'd never seen himself—or allowed himself to see.

"Scarlett," he said, automatically returning his sister's hug, "there are no sparks. I told you it's a marriage of convenience."

"Yeah, I heard you," she countered and gave his cheek a pat as she straightened up. "Doesn't mean I believe you. I've seen the way you look at Naomi, Toby. And it's not like you're thinking *hey, good buddy.*"

"That's exactly what it is. She's my friend. That's all."

Shaking her head, Scarlett glanced at the wall clock and said, "If that's how you want to play it, fine. Look, I've got to run. There's a cow giving birth, and if she manages to pull it off before I get there, people will think they don't need to call me for this stuff." She grabbed her huge black leather bag and headed for the back door.

Once there, she stopped, ran her fingers through her short honey-brown hair and narrowed wide hazel eyes on him. "But I'll want more details later, you hear? 'Bye, Mom. Don't know when I'll be back."

And she was gone. Scarlett McKittrick was a force of nature, Toby thought, not for the first time. She'd always moved through life like a whirlwind, and now that she was a vet, it was even worse. Answering calls for help at all hours, she was dedicated to the animals she loved and as caring as their mother.

Scarlett did everything at a dead run, moving from patient to patient and keeping a grin on her face while she was doing it. Most people looked at her and thought she was too slight to do the kind of work she did. But Toby had seen his sister in action. When one of his mares got into trouble during labor, Scarlett had been there to save the foal and the mother. He knew she had the strength, determination and pure stubbornness to do a job most often thought to be a man's purview.

When the door slammed behind her, silence settled on the homey kitchen. He glanced around quickly while he grabbed a chocolate chip cookie from the plate in the middle of the table. The walls were sky blue and the cabinets were painted bright white. Toby himself had painted the kitchen for his mother the summer before, and he figured she'd be ready for another change by next year. The floor was wide oak planks, and the fridge and the stove had been replaced with top-of-the-line new ones. But there were old pictures attached with magnets to the new fridge, and when he looked at the images of him and Scarlett as kids, he had to smile. His mom's old mutt, Lola, was napping on a cushion under the bay window, and her snores rattled in the room.

Toby had grown up in this house and spent too many hours to count sitting at this very table. He'd done his homework here, had family dinners, come in late from a date to find his mother awake and waiting up for him. So it made sense to him that it was here that he and his mother had the conversation he could see building in her eyes.

Joyce McKittrick was short, with golden-blond hair that fell in waves to her shoulders. Her blue eyes were as sharp as ever, and she never missed a thing. She was, he thought, beautiful, strong and smart. Hadn't she stepped up when Toby's father died, to raise Scarlett and him on her own? Thanks to her husband's life insurance, they hadn't had to worry about money, but Joyce had never been one to sit back and do nothing. She'd boarded horses and given riding lessons to local kids. And she'd encouraged both Scarlett's love of animals and Toby's inventive nature. In fact, she was the one who'd made sure he got a patent on his very first invention—a robotic ketchup dispenser he'd come up with at the age of ten.

Joyce was his touchstone, the heart of their family, and she had given his sister and him the kind of home life that Naomi had missed out on.

"When you first said you were marrying Naomi, I was pleased. She's a good person, and I'm glad she's finally letting that side of her out to shine instead of hiding behind a mean streak that wasn't natural to her."

He smiled to himself. Trust Joyce to see past the surface to the truth beneath. Not many had, really. Naomi, Cecelia and Simone had been like a trio of mean for a long time. They had always seemed to enjoy setting people back a step. To strike quick with a sharp word or a hard look.

But times, like everything else, changed, and now the three of them seemed to be coming into their own. Naomi, especially, he thought, had done well by letting go of her past enough to carve out the future she wanted for herself.

"Should have known you'd see through all that drama she used to be a part of," Toby said ruefully.

"Of course I did." Joyce waved that aside. "Her parents are…difficult and they made Naomi's life a misery for her, I know. It says something about her character that she's come so far all on her own." She reached out and smoothed his hair back from his face. "Though she had a good friend, these last few years, to be there for her."

"I have been," Toby said, wanting her to understand. "And I'm going to continue."

"I know that, too," his mother said, sitting back in her chair to give him a long look. "But, Toby, starting a marriage with a lie isn't the best way to go."

"We're not lying to each other," he countered. "Or to you and Scarlett." He'd known she'd feel this way, and he couldn't blame her. But he could convince her he knew what he was doing. "Naomi needs me, Mom. That baby does, too. I watched you struggle as a single mother, and I don't want to watch Naomi do the same. We get along great. We're good friends."

Apparently with sparks, he warned himself silently, and then dismissed the warning. "We're good together, and this is what I want."

"Then I want it for you," she said, though her eyes said different. "All I ask is that you be careful. That you really think about what you're letting yourself in for."

He grinned and winked. "I'm always careful."

"Not nearly enough," she said, laughing a little.

"Honestly," Toby said, stealing another cookie and taking a bite. No one made cookies like Joyce McKittrick. "I figured you'd have the most trouble with me claiming the baby as mine."

"Not a bit," she said, shaking her head firmly. "That baby is an innocent, and you and Naomi are doing the right thing for it. I just want to be sure it's the right thing for *you*."

"It is, Mom," he said, his tone deep and serious. "I never figured to get married..."

She snorted a laugh. "Men always seem to say that, yet the world is filled with husbands."

His eyebrows arched. "*Anyway*," he said pointedly, "Naomi and I are good together. I think we'll make this work for all of us."

"I always liked Naomi," Joyce said, nodding. "She's got a lot of spirit and a little sass, and that's a good thing. But she's also got a heart that's not been treated very gently over the years."

"I'm not going to hurt her."

"Not purposely, of course," she said. "And she wouldn't intentionally hurt you, either. Still, I'm your mother, so I'll worry a little, and there's nothing either of us can do to stop that. But if it's my blessing you were after, you have it."

"You're amazing," he said softly.

"I just know my son." She stood up, walked to a cupboard and came back with a plastic zip bag. She dumped every last cookie into the bag and sealed it before handing it over to Toby. "You take these home with you. And when you get home, you have a good long talk with yourself. Make sure this is what you want."

"I have. I will." He reached out and patted her hand. "I know what I'm doing."

Joyce shook her head and smiled wryly. "Scarlett was right, you know. There's always been sparks between you and Naomi."

"Mom…"

"I'm just saying, don't be surprised if those sparks kindle a fire neither of you is expecting."

Four

The next morning, Naomi was at the local cable studio outside Royal. No matter what else was going on in her life, she had a job to do—the fact that she loved her job was a bonus.

The station was small but had everything you could need. Local businesses used it to film commercials, the high school football games were broadcast from the studio, and Naomi's own show had been born there. The studio was so well set up they had community college students as interns, helping the professional staff.

She tried to focus on the upcoming taping of her show, but it wasn't easy to concentrate when she knew that Toby would be coming by her condo that afternoon to help move her things to the ranch.

Naomi stopped on the walk across the parking lot, just to allow her brain to wheel through everything that was happening. She'd worked hard to buy her little condo in Royal and then to fix it up just as she wanted it. Sure, it was small, but it was *hers*. Her own place. And now she was giving it up to move to the country.

Granted, growing up in a small town in Texas, she was used to being in the country. But she'd never *lived* there. And not only was she giving up her home, but she was marrying her best friend, and that still was enough to make her bite her bottom lip and question herself.

In fact, Naomi had spent most of the night before pacing through her home, mind spinning. Was she doing the right thing? She didn't know. There were plenty of doubts, plenty of questions and not many answers. All she could be sure of was the decision had been made and there was no backing out now—since the whole town was talking about her engagement to Toby.

Of course, she told herself, since everyone was busy with Toby's lie, no one was talking much about the hideous video Maverick had put out. And today she was taping her first maternity-wear show—fighting fire with fire. Maverick had wanted to make her look foolish, but she would take his announcement and make it her own. Toby had been right about that. If Maverick wanted her crying in a corner somewhere, he was going to be really disappointed.

Truthfully, it was a relief to no longer have to hide the fact that she was pregnant. Disguising a growing baby bump wasn't easy. Loose shirts, pinned slacks and an oversize bag to hold in front of the rounding part of her body could only work for so long. Knowing her secret was out was…liberating in a way she hadn't expected.

Taking a deep breath, she headed for the building, stepped into the air-conditioned cool and came face-to-face with Eddie, the lead cameraman. He was an older man, with grizzled salt-and-pepper hair that stuck out around his head like he'd been electrocuted.

"We're ready for the run-through, Naomi." He gave her a smile and a thumbs-up. "You good to go?"

"I really am, as soon as I stop by makeup," she said. Twenty minutes later, she walked to the set, hair perfect, makeup just as she wanted it and her wardrobe displaying that bump she'd been hiding for too long.

Local cable channel or not, Naomi's show, *Fashion Sense*, was catching on. In the last year, she'd managed to get picked up by affiliates in Houston and Dallas, and just this week a station in Galveston had contacted her about carrying her show. And, thanks to social media, word about her show was spreading far beyond the Texas borders. Her Facebook page boasted followers from as far away as New York and California and even a few in Europe.

Naomi had plans. She wanted to take her show national. She wanted to be featured in magazines, to be taken seriously enough that even her parents would have to sit up and take notice. And she was going to make those dreams come true. Lifting her chin, Naomi walked in long, determined strides to the center of her set and turned to face the camera and her growing audience. The lights were bright, hot and felt absolutely right.

"In five, four," Tammy, the assistant sound engineer, said, counting down with her fingers as well until she reached one and pointed at Naomi.

"Hi, and welcome to *Fashion Sense*. I'm Naomi Price." She was comfortable in front of the camera. Always had been, a small part of her mind admitted quietly. Toby had been right about that, too. She enjoyed being the center of attention when it was *her* idea.

And she had a lot of ideas. Just last night, while she wandered her condo hoping for sleep, her mind had raced with all kinds of possibilities. To grow her audience, she had to grow the show itself. Make it appeal to as many people as possible. There were plenty of women out there, she knew, who didn't give a damn about fashion—though she found that hard to believe. But those women did care about their homes, decorating. Just look at all the DIY programs that were so popular.

Well, she couldn't build a staircase or install fresh lighting, but she knew how to find those who could. So today, she was going to announce a few of the changes she had in mind. Starting, she told herself, with the biggest announcement of all. With Maverick's video out and viral by now, she had to assume that her viewers had seen it, or would have by the time this show aired. So she was taking control of the situation.

"As you can see," she said, turning sideways to show off the baby bump proudly displayed beneath a tight lavender tank, "my own personal fashion style will be undergoing some drastic transformations over the next few months. My fiancé, Toby McKittrick, and I are both very happy about our coming baby and we're excited to greet all the new things in our future."

Smiling into the camera, she faced the audience head-on again and continued. "And to keep up with the changes in my life, I'm going to be doing a lot of shows focusing on contemporary, fashionable maternity wear, obviously."

Again, that brilliant smile shot into the camera and into homes across Texas. "But don't worry. It's not going to be all babies all the time. As our lives grow and evolve, we have to keep up. So here on *Fashion Sense*, we're going to be branching out—dipping into home furnishings and gardens and even designing your own outdoor living space." She tossed her hair back from her face and winked. "Since I'm expanding, I thought it was only right the show did a little growing, too."

Off camera, she heard a chuckle from one of the grips and knew she'd hit just the right note.

"So I hope you'll come with me on this journey of discovery. Over the next few months, we'll all be in new territory—should be fun!"

"And cut."

When Eddie gave her the go-ahead, Naomi looked at him and asked, "Well, how'd I do?"

"Great, Naomi, seriously great." Eddie winked at her. "I think you're on to something with this house stuff. My wife's always watching those home shows, coming up with things for me to do. So I already know she'll be hounding me to do whatever it is you show her."

"Good to know," Naomi said, laughing.

"We're gonna set up for the next shot. Be about fifteen minutes," Eddie said as the crew scurried around, making TV magic happen.

As long as most women felt as Eddie's wife did, this new direction Naomi was determined to take would work out. All she had to do was bring in experts to interview and to demonstrate their specialties. She could already see it. Gardeners, painters, tiling specialists. She would push *Fashion Sense* to the next level—and at the bottom of it, didn't she have Maverick to thank for the push?

Unsettling thought. Naomi wandered off to a chair in a quiet corner of the studio, sat down and turned her phone on. She checked her email, sighed a little at the number of them and wondered halfheartedly how many of them were because of Maverick's video. With that thought in mind, she closed her email program. She didn't need to deal with them right this minute, and she really didn't want to ruin the good mood she was in.

Because she felt great. She'd taken Maverick's slap at her and turned it around. She was taking ownership of her pregnancy, pushing her show to new heights—and marrying her best friend.

Okay, she could admit that she was still worried about that. Toby had been such an important part of her life for so long that if she lost him because of a fake marriage, it would break her heart. So maybe they needed to talk again. To really think this through, together. To somehow make a pact that their friendship would always come first.

The rumble and scrape of furniture being moved echoed in the building, letting her know the guys were still hard at work. So when her phone rang, Naomi checked the screen and felt her heart sink into a suddenly open pit in her stomach.

Wouldn't you know it? Just when things were starting to look up.

Answering her phone, she said, "Hello, Gio."

"Ciao, *bella*." The voice was smooth, dark and warm, just as she remembered it from that night nearly five months ago now.

Naomi closed her eyes as the memory swept over her, and she shook her head to lose it again just as fast. It wasn't easy admitting that you'd been stupid enough to have a one-night stand with a man you *knew* would be nothing more than that. And even though they'd used protection, apparently it wasn't foolproof.

Gio Fabiani, gorgeous, lying player who'd sneaked past her defenses long enough to get her into bed. Even now Naomi felt a quick stab of regret for her own poor choices. But moaning over the past wouldn't get her anywhere. She opened her eyes, looked across the room at the crew busily working and kept her voice low as she spoke to Gio. As much as she'd prefer to just hang up on the man, she had to do the right thing and tell him about the baby.

"I have your many messages on my phone, *bella*," Gio was saying. "What is so important? Is it that you miss me?"

She rolled her eyes and ground her teeth together, silently praying for patience. Behind his voice, she heard the telltale clatter and noise of a busy restaurant. With the time difference between Texas and Italy, it was late afternoon for Gio and he was probably at his favorite trattoria, sitting at a table on the sidewalk where he could see and be seen. She frowned at the mental image and then instantly shut down everything but the urge to get the truth said and done.

"I've been trying to get hold of you for months, Gio," she said softly.

"*Sì, sì,* I have been very busy."

Getting other foolish women into his bed, no doubt, and oh, how it burned to know she'd been just one of a crowd.

"Yes, me too. Gio," she said, taking a breath to say it all at once. "I'm pregnant."

Silence on the other end of the line and then, "This is happy news for you, *si*?"

She skipped right over that. None of his business how she was feeling. "You're the father."

A longer silence from him this time, and she heard the street sounds of Italy in the background. She could see him, lounging in a chair, legs kicked out in front of him, a glass of wine in one hand and the phone in the other. What she couldn't see was his reaction. She didn't have long to wait for it, though.

"I am no one's father, *bella*," he said softly enough that she had to strain to hear him. "If you carry the baby, the baby is yours, not mine."

She hadn't expected anything else, but still, hearing it felt like a slap. How many women, she wondered, had made this call to Gio? How many times had he heard about a child he'd made just before he walked away from all responsibility? He was a dog, but it was her own fault that she'd fallen for his practiced charm. Toby had been right about him, of course. He'd called him a user, and that described Gio to a tee.

Naomi didn't actually *want* Gio in her life or her baby's. It seemed she would get what she wanted. But she had to be sure they both understood right where things were. "You're not interested?"

"*Bella*, you must see that I am not a man who wishes the encumbrance of a child."

The tone of his voice was that of a man trying to explain something to a very stupid person. And maybe she had been stupid. Once. But she wasn't anymore.

"That's fine, Gio. I'm not the one who made this phone call, Gio. I don't want anything from you," she said, flicking a glance toward the set, making sure no one was within earshot. "You had a right to know about the baby. That's it."

"Ah," he said on a long sigh of what she assumed was satisfaction. "Then we are finished together, yes?"

Big yes, she thought. In an instant, her mind drew up an image of Toby and what had happened yesterday. How he'd stood with her to face her parents. The difference between the two men was incalculable. Toby would always do the right thing. Always. Gio did the expedient thing. And Naomi herself? She would do what was best for her baby. And that was ridding them of the man who was, as he'd pointed out, *no one's* father.

"Yes, Gio," she said, her grip on the phone tightening until her fingers ached. "We're finished."

And she was relieved. She'd never have to see him or deal with him again. There was no worry about him coming back at some later date, wanting to be a part of her baby's life. The minute he hung up the phone, Gio would forget all about this conversation. He would forget *her*. And that was best for everybody.

"*Arrivederci, bella,*" Gio said and, without waiting for a response from her, disconnected.

She expelled a breath, looked at her phone for a long minute, then shook her head. Naomi had been trying to reach Gio for weeks, and when she finally did manage a conversation with him, it had lasted about three minutes. It felt as if a huge weight had been lifted off her shoulders. "It's over."

Of course it had *been* over for months. Heck, it had never even started with Gio, really. You couldn't count one night as anything other than a blip on the radar that appeared and disappeared in the blink of an eye. If she hadn't gotten pregnant, would she even have given Gio a single thought? "No, I wouldn't have," she said out loud.

Really, she'd have done everything possible to never think about one night of bad judgment. She looked down at the phone in her hand as a wave of relief swept over her. Gio was well and truly out of her life. Naomi knew Toby would be pleased to hear it.

Toby.

The familiar noises of the crew working registered in one part of her mind as her thoughts swirled as if caught in a tornado. What did it say, she asked herself, that the first person she wanted to tell about the call from Gio was Toby? That he was her best friend. That he was the one person in her life she always turned to first.

Maybe marrying him would be all right, she told herself now. Maybe it would be good for all of them.

She trusted him, she loved him—as a friend—and she knew she'd always be able to count on him. So what was she so worried about? No sex? Not that big a deal, she assured herself silently. Heck, it wasn't as if pregnant women had red-hot sex lives anyway.

Was it fair to Toby? Wasn't that up to him? she reasoned. If he wanted to marry her, why shouldn't she? Yes, she could be a single mother. She was perfectly capable of raising a child on her own. But as Toby had pointed out, why deliberately take the hard route when there was another answer? And knowing that Toby would be with her, sharing it all, seemed to make the niggling fears of impending motherhood easier to conquer. But what to do with the fears she had of losing her best friend because of a convenient lie?

"We're ready, Naomi," Tammy shouted from across the room.

Pushing herself out of the chair, still wrestling with her thoughts, Naomi walked to the set. Distracted, she took her place in the center of the stage.

"Hey, hey," Eddie said. "Find your smile again, Naomi. We've got to finish this segment."

"Right." She shook off the dark thoughts, focused again on the moment and resolved to put all her energies into making this the best show she could.

Toby led the way into the stable, glancing over his shoulder at Clay Everett. As a former rodeo champ, Clay was the best judge of horseflesh in the county—

not counting Toby himself, of course. Clay had left the rodeo behind after a bull-riding accident that had been bad enough to leave him with a slight limp. And a part of the man still missed it, Toby knew. The competition, the intensity of a seven-second ride that could win a trophy or break your heart. But he was settled now in Royal on his own ranch, and horses were still a big part of his life.

Of course there was more to Clay than being a successful rancher. His company, Everest, installed cloud infrastructure for corporations and was in demand by everyone with half a brain. Though Clay was a hell of a businessman, his heart was still at his ranch. The man was much like Toby in that way. Didn't matter how many inventions Toby came up with or how his business interests ate up his time, the ranch fed his soul.

There were twenty stalls in Toby's stables, but only eleven of them were occupied at the moment. Clay was here to see one of Toby's treasures—a beautiful chestnut mare called Rain.

"I brought her in from the south pasture this morning. Thought you'd want to take a close look at her before sealing the deal."

"You thought right," Clay said and stopped alongside Toby at the stall's half door. Inside the enclosure, the beautiful horse stood idly nosing at the fresh straw on the floor. When Toby clucked his tongue, the mare looked up, then moved to greet him.

"She's a beauty," Clay said, reaching out to stroke the flat of his hand along the horse's neck.

The mare actually seemed to preen under the attention. Clay laughed. "Yeah, you know you're something special, don't you?"

"She does." Toby watched Clay feed the mare an apple he'd brought along just for that reason. "She's two years old, good health—Scarlett did a full physical on her last week."

"Scarlett's word's good enough for me," Clay said, stroking the horse's nose. "Yeah, you still want to sell her, I want her."

"Deal," Toby said and gave the mare one longing look. Raising horses also meant you had to sell them, too. You couldn't keep them all. But every time he sold a horse, he felt the loss like a physical pang. Still, he knew Clay would be good to her, and Toby would get a chance to see her once in a while.

"We'll go up to the house, have a beer and take care of business."

"Sounds good," Clay said. Then he slanted Toby a look. "I hear you and Naomi are getting married."

Getting married. The words didn't send a clawing sense of dread and panic ripping through him. After Sasha walked out on him, Toby had pulled back from anything even remotely resembling a relationship. Now here he was, engaged, going to be a father, and it felt...good.

Toby blew out a breath, tipped the brim of his Stetson back a bit and nodded. Here it was. He was

going to look into his friend's eyes and lie to him.
But, hell. A lie to protect Naomi didn't bother him
a bit. "When you've got a baby coming, it's time to
get married."

Clay's eyebrows lifted. "Hadn't heard the baby
part of the rumor. My source is slipping."

Toby grinned. "Times are sad when you can't
count on the gossip chain to be thorough."

"Can't believe how the men in this town are getting caught in the marriage trap." Clay shook his
head as if very sad for all his friends. The man's
smile, though, told Toby he was enjoying all this.
"Wes Jackson is a man I thought would never go
down that road, and look at him now."

Toby had been thinking the same thing just a
few months ago. Watching Wes reconnect with the
woman he loved and discover he had a daughter had
hit Toby hard at the time. Back then he'd felt the same
way Clay did now, that somehow Wes had set himself
up for pain. Funny how your ideas could change so
dramatically in just a few months. Of course, he reminded himself, he wasn't in love with Naomi. This
was a bargain between friends. Which was why it
would work.

"He's happy." Toby braced both feet wide apart,
folding his arms across his chest. Just because he
wasn't looking for love didn't mean he couldn't recognize it when he saw it. "Hell, he practically *glows*
when he's around Belle. And as for his daughter,
Caro, he's become such a whiz at sign language he's

talking about teaching it to a few of us so we can talk secretly to each other in the TCC board meetings."

Sunlight speared through the open stable doors, pouring spears of gold into the shadowy interior. The building smelled of horses and hay—one of Toby's favorite scents.

Nodding thoughtfully, Clay said, "Not a bad plan there. But not the point of what I was saying. It's this whole wedding plague that's sweeping through Royal. It's picking the men off one by one."

"A *plague*?" Toby laughed.

"It sure as hell seems contagious," Clay said. Ticking them off on his fingers, he continued. "There's Deacon and Hutch and Tom Knox."

"Tom doesn't count," Toby interrupted. "He and Emily were already married."

"Yeah, but they were separated, now they're not," Clay pointed out. "Then there's Shane and now *you*."

Toby laughed shortly and shook his head. "I'm not sick—so not contagious, no worries there. I'm not caught in a trap, either, man. I'm marrying my best friend." And as he said it, Toby again felt the rightness of it. There was no risk in this marriage. No worry about falling for a woman and having her walk out, taking half his heart with her.

He'd already done that. Already lived through betrayal and having his heart smashed under the boot of a woman who decided some loser wannabe country singer was a better bet than a Texas inventor/cowboy. When Sasha walked out, she'd burned him badly enough that Toby hadn't wanted anything to do with women. But Naomi had been there with him, through all of it.

He didn't give a damn about Sasha anymore and figured he'd made a lucky escape in spite of the pain and fury he'd survived. And Naomi had helped him get clear of all that. So marrying her was not just a perfect solution to the current problem—it was also a way to stand by Naomi. To thank her for being there for him when he needed it most. This marriage meant he got his best friend living with him. He got a child to raise and love, and he didn't have to worry about whether or not he could trust his wife.

"Yeah, well," Clay said wryly, "she's your best friend *now*. That'll stop when she's your *wife*."

A flicker of doubt sputtered into life inside him, but Toby squashed it flat. "Not Naomi. I trust her."

"Your funeral," Clay said with a shrug.

"You talk a hard game," Toby retorted with a half laugh. "But then there's Sophie."

Sophie Prescott. Clay's secretary.

The other man shrugged, stuffed his hands into his pockets and said, "What about her?"

"Oh, man, don't try to look innocent. You can't pull it off." Toby laughed. "I've seen the way you look at her."

"Looking's one thing. Marrying's another," Clay allowed with a grin. "The rest of you may get picked off one by one, but you can bank on me being the last single man standing."

"Yeah," Toby said, heading for the house, waiting for Clay to follow, "that's what we all say. But you know what? You're going back to a cold, empty ranch, while I'll be here with Naomi."

He smiled to himself as he realized he was looking forward to having her here. To her being a part of his everyday life. Of watching that baby inside her grow. With Naomi, he could have the life he wanted with none of the dangers or risks. What man wouldn't want that?

Five

"So," Simone asked as she set an empty box down on Naomi's bed, "how excited is Toby to be a father?"

Simone had her nearly blue-black hair pulled back into a thick tail that hung down between her shoulder blades. The woman's amazing ice-blue eyes shone with a kind of happiness Naomi was glad to see there. Simone had the kind of face that made most people think she was gorgeous but empty-headed. It didn't take her long to prove just how brilliant she really was.

"He says he's really happy about it." Which was true, but not the whole truth. A flicker of unease rippled through her as Naomi realized that to keep her bargain with Toby, keep her baby safe, she'd have to lie to her closest friends.

It wasn't that she didn't trust Simone and Cecelia both. They'd been friends forever, and heaven knew the three of them had shared so many secrets, there really wasn't much they didn't know about each other. But she had to think about her baby, too. The baby who would grow up knowing Toby as its father. Was it fair to her child to let other people in on the fact that Gio Fabiani had been her sperm donor? And that was really all he had been, she assured herself. He wasn't a father in any sense of the word, so did he really deserve to even be mentioned? Now that she'd actually spoken to him and knew without a doubt that he'd never have anything to do with the baby, wasn't it better for everyone to just forget about his involvement completely?

"I can't believe you managed to keep your pregnancy a secret. From *us*," Simone added. "I mean, you're nearly five months, right?"

"It's because she never eats," Cecelia put in, playfully sticking her tongue out at Naomi. She was any man's dream woman, Naomi thought. Gray-green eyes, long wavy platinum hair, a curvy figure and long legs. She was also driven, ambitious and funny. "She's pregnant and still skinnier than I am."

Skinny. That had been Naomi's goal for most of her life. Now her body would be doing as much changing as her life, and she found she wasn't too concerned about it. Maybe it was having Toby stand-

ing with her. Maybe it was finally accepting and
being proud of the fact that she was going to be a
mother. Whatever the reason, though, Naomi thought
it was about time she stopped worrying so much
about the scale. She had more to think of than herself
now, right? Hadn't Toby said just the other day that
the baby needed more than a lettuce leaf to grow on?

"Naomi?" Cecelia asked. "You okay?"

"What? Yeah. Sorry. I'm fine. I'm just—" She
paused, looked around at the chaos strewn around the
bedroom of her condo and realized it was the perfect
metaphor for her life. "Overwhelmed."

"Easy to understand," Simone said, folding another sweater and laying it in a box. "It's not every
day you get slammed in a viral video, get engaged
and announce a pregnancy."

"God," Naomi whispered. "It sounds even crazier
when you say it out loud."

"Yes, but you're handling it," Cecelia said, pushing her hair back and kicking back onto the bed to
get comfy. She crossed her feet at the ankle, grabbed
a pillow and held it against her belly. "Simone and I
have had our share of crazy lately, too, remember?"

"Absolutely," Simone muttered and pushed Cecelia's feet out of the way to reach for a stack of folded
T-shirts. "Honestly, I didn't know what was going to
happen with Deacon, but now look at us."

Cecelia tossed Simone more shirts while Naomi
zipped her cosmetics case closed.

"Heck, look at *all* of us," Cecelia said with a wide

smile. "The mean girls are done, and we're all in love."

Naomi sighed a little.

"Plus," Cecelia added, "we're all pregnant at the same time. Our kids can grow up friends."

"I'm more pregnant," Simone pointed out. "There's three in here." She patted her slightly rounded tummy. "Remember?"

Cecelia laughed. "You always were a show-off."

Naomi smiled, too, because it was so easy to be with these women. They'd been a trio for so long she couldn't even imagine her life without them in it. She had great friends. Cecelia, Simone—and Toby.

Bottom line, worries and all, it came down to the fact that she was marrying her best friend. How bad could it be?

"Is it time for a break?" Cecelia asked from the bed. "Come on, let's let the new fiancé finish this up when he gets here."

"Cec," Simone said, "if you'd pack as much as you talk, we'd be finished by now."

"Talking's more fun," Cecelia said, but she dutifully pushed herself off the bed, walked to the closet and dragged Naomi's garment bag down off the high shelf. "Fine. I'll get as much of her stuff into this thing as I can. But there's no way we'll get all your clothes in one trip, Naomi."

"I know." Her condo was small, but the closets were huge. It was really what had sold her on the place. "You know what?" she said, making up her mind on the spot. "Cec, do what you can with that bag. Simone, when we fill up this box, we're stopping. That's it. I've got enough to live on, and it's not like I'm moving to the moon. Toby and I can come back to get the rest another time."

"Deal. I feel ice cream coming on," Cecelia said from the depths of the closet.

Simone sighed. "Ice cream. I love ice cream. And I'm going to be *much* bigger than you guys will be, so I shouldn't have any. But I'm weak."

"You're safe, then," Naomi told her with a shrug. "I don't have ice cream in the house." In fact, she didn't have anything fattening in the condo. She'd never seen the point in testing her own willpower.

"Oh, that's just wrong." Cecelia came out of the closet, laid the garment bag on the bed, then picked up her purse. "I'm going up to the store for ice cream and maybe cookies. I'll be back in fifteen minutes."

When she was gone, Simone said, "Thank goodness for Cec. I really do want ice cream now."

Naomi laughed. "I guess we do have to have some priorities, huh?"

"Ice cream is top of the list," Simone said. Then she hooked one arm around Naomi's shoulders. "I know what you're thinking. Everything's changing."

"Yeah," Naomi agreed, wrapping one arm around her friend's waist, "that's it exactly."

"I was feeling the same way just a few weeks ago, but then I remembered the most important thing."

"What's that?" Naomi asked.

"Change can be *good*, too."

"You're right," Naomi said and looked around the room again.

This condo had been perfect for her once. When she was single, with nothing more to think about than the career she was trying to forge. But the condo wasn't who she was anymore.

It was time to figure out who she was becoming.

"We can't sleep in the same bed."

Later that night, Naomi was at Paradise Ranch, staring up at Toby in stunned surprise. Sure, they had a no-sex agreement, but *look* at him.

He took a breath and blew it out again in obvious exasperation. "Naomi, you know I've got a house-keeper. If Rebecca sees we're not staying in the same room, how long do you figure it'll be before the rest of Royal knows it?"

"But—" She looked at the gigantic bed against the far wall of Toby's bedroom and shook her head. Sure, it was big enough for four or five people, but was it big enough for the two of them?

The room was cavernous, just right for the master of the house. There was a black granite fireplace tall enough for Naomi to stand up in, with two chairs and a table sitting in front of the now cold hearth. Along one wall were bookcases stuffed with hard- and soft-backed books, family pictures, and framed patents Toby had received for his many inventions. Across from the bed, a gigantic flat-screen TV hung on the wall, and French doors on the far wall led out to a wide wooden balcony that overlooked the fields behind the house and the really spectacular pool.

But her gaze kept sliding back to that bed. A massive four-poster, with heavy head- and footboards, the mattress was covered in a dark red quilt that looked as if it had been hand stitched. Toby's mother, Joyce, was a quilting fiend, so she was probably behind that. And there was a small mountain of pillows propped against that headboard, practically begging a person to climb up and sink in.

The whole room was inviting, and Naomi had to at least partially blame herself for that, since she'd helped him decorate the house. But she'd never imagined herself sleeping in the master bedroom.

"I thought I'd be staying in one of the guest rooms," she argued. "You've got seven bedrooms in this place."

"Yeah." He scrubbed one hand across the beard stubble on his jaw. "But married people sleep together. That's what folks expect."

He had a point, and why hadn't she considered it before? She hadn't counted on this at all. How was she supposed to share a bed with her best friend?

"Okay, look," he said, clearly reading what she was thinking. "We'll try this. You can sleep in the room next to mine, but all your stuff stays here, in my room. That should throw Rebecca off the scent. Especially if we keep that guest room looking like nobody's been in it."

"Okay. I can do that." This was crazy and getting worse by the minute. Enforced closeness was going to push their friendship places it had never been before, and it really worried her that the relationship might just snap from all the tension.

Reaching out for him, she laid one hand on his forearm and waited until his gaze shifted to hers. "You have to promise me, Toby. You have to swear that no matter what else happens between us, we stay friends."

"That's not even a question, Naomi." He pulled her in close for a hard hug, and Naomi surprised herself by leaning into him, relishing the feel of his strength wrapping itself around her. So much was changing so quickly that he was her stable point in the universe, and if she lost him, Naomi didn't think she could take it.

"We're gonna do fine, Naomi. Don't worry." His hands moved up and down her back, and tiny whips of heat sneaked beneath her defenses. Startled by that simmering burn, she stepped away from him, told herself that she was just tired. Distracted. Vulnerable. But that heat was still there, and Naomi knew she needed some distance.

And she didn't think the guest room was going to be far enough away.

Naomi hadn't been awake at 6:00 a.m. in...*ever*. And couldn't understand why she was now.

An avowed town girl, Naomi had always believed

the only reason to be up with the sun was that your house was on fire. Yet now she was going to be a rancher's wife. She was in the country, where the quiet was so profound it was almost alive. There were no cars roaring down the street, no neighbors with a too-loud stereo. Here the night was really dark and there were more stars in the sky than she'd ever known existed.

She hadn't slept well, either. Lying there in the dark, listening to the quiet, knowing Toby was just on the other side of the wall, had kept her too on edge to do more than doze on and off. So this morning, it was too early, she was too sleepy and felt too off balance. Clutching the single measly cup of coffee she allowed herself each day she stepped out onto the back porch, where the soft, morning breeze slid past her.

The only reason she was up early enough to watch the sun claim the sky and begin to beat down on Texas with a vengeance was that Toby had woken her in the guest room so she could move into his bedroom while he went to work.

Once in Toby's bed, she'd tried to get back to sleep, but the pillows carried his scent and the sheets were still warm from his skin, and none of that was conducive to sleeping. She could have stayed upstairs and unpacked, but instead she'd grabbed one of Toby's T-shirts and pulled it on over her maternity jeans—that thankfully didn't *look* like maternity jeans unless you saw the elastic panel over the belly. She wore slip-on red sneakers and left her hair to hang in a tumble over her shoulders.

Now she looked around in the early morning heat and thought how beautiful Paradise Ranch was. There were live oaks studding the yard, providing patches of shade under the already blazing Texas sun. A kitchen garden behind the house was laid out in tidy rows and surrounded by a low white picket fence in the hopes of discouraging rabbits. The corral was enclosed by a high fence, also painted white, and the barn as well as the bunkhouse used by the cowboys who worked for Toby were freshly painted in a deep brick red. Toby's workshop was on the other side of the property from the barn and was the same farm-yard red as the rest of the outbuildings.

The yard in front of the house boasted a neatly tended green lawn. Summer flowers in bright jewel tones hugged the base of the big house. But the house itself was the masterpiece. Two stories, it was the kind of house you expected to see in a mountain setting, with cedar walls, river rocks along the foundation and tall windows that opened the house up to wide views of the ranchland. To one side of the house was a pool, surrounded by rocks and waterfalls so cleverly designed that it looked like a naturally formed lagoon, and the whole thing was shaded by more oaks and a vine-covered pergola. A wrap-around porch held tables and comfortable chairs that signaled a welcome and silently invited people to sit and relax.

This wasn't her first visit to Toby's ranch. She'd helped him design it. Helped to decorate it. Yet it all felt…different to her now. Not surprising, she told herself, since now she was *living* here. And awake way too early.

She took another sip of her coffee and let her gaze slide across the trees, the field beyond the barn and then back to the corral where Toby was grooming one of his prized horses.

Toby stood near the fence, brushing down a golden-brown horse whose coat seemed to shine in the sunlight. But as beautiful as the horse was, Naomi couldn't take her eyes off Toby. He wasn't wearing a shirt. She took another gulp of coffee and struggled to swallow past the knot in her throat.

His chest was broad and chiseled, skin tanned, and every move he made had his muscles rippling in a way that made her think of those cool sheets and the wide bed.

"Oh, God…" Hormones, she told herself. Had to be hormones running amok inside her. Pregnancy was making her crazy. It was the only explanation for why looking at her best friend could suddenly turn her insides to mush.

She laid one hand on her rounded belly, and touching her baby seemed to ground her. Remind her of why she was here. What she'd agreed to. And for heaven's sake, Toby was her *friend*. She had no business getting all ruffled over a muscular chest and a tight butt encased in worn blue denim. She shouldn't even be noticing how the shadows thrown across his features by his cowboy hat made his face look sharply dangerous. And if she had any sense at all, she'd turn right around and go back in the house.

"Naomi?"

Oh, thank God. She turned to the open back door where Rebecca stood, holding out a sturdy wicker basket. "Yes?"

Rebecca had graying red hair, bottle-green eyes and freckles sprinkled liberally across her nose and cheeks. She was a widow in her midfifties with two grown kids who lived in Houston. She'd been working for Toby for five years and lived in a set of rooms off the kitchen. And she couldn't be more excited at the prospect of having a baby in the house to take care of.

"I've got to get breakfast going, and you could do me a huge favor if you'd go collect some eggs for me."

"Eggs?"

Rebecca wiggled the basket. "The chicken coop is on the other side of the barn. Just gather what's there. Should be enough with what's still in the fridge."

Naomi walked over, took the basket and handed her now-empty coffee cup to the other woman. "You know, I've never actually gathered eggs before," she admitted, wondering why it sounded like an apology.

"Nothing to it." Rebecca was already darting back into the coolness of the house. "Just reach under the chickens and grab them up." She let the screen door slam behind her, then closed the wood door as well.

"Reach under the chickens." Naomi looked at the empty basket, then lifted her gaze to the side of the barn where she could just make out another structure. A chicken coop. With chickens in it. Did chickens bite?

"I guess I'll find out," she muttered and started walking. If nothing else, this should take her mind off Toby. For now, anyway. She was headed across the yard, in no hurry to find out what *reaching under a chicken* was like, when Toby's voice stopped her.

"Hey, Naomi, come on over here a minute."

She changed course and walked to the corral, swinging the wicker basket with each step. Toby watched her approach, and even in the shadow of his hat, she saw those aqua eyes of his shining. Then Toby flashed a grin that made her heartbeat jolt a little, and Naomi told herself to get a grip.

Honestly, she'd always known he was a good-looking man. You'd have to be blind not to notice. But did he have to be *gorgeous*? Up close, his chest looked broader, his skin tanner, and every muscle seemed to have been carved out of bronze. She swallowed hard, forced a smile and said, "I'm supposed to be gathering eggs. Do the chickens mind?"

He laughed.

"Seriously," she said. "How do you gather eggs?"

Shaking his head, he said, "You're a smart woman. You'll figure it out." Toby opened the corral gate so she could step into the paddock with him. "I wanted you to meet Legend."

The horse he held by the bridle was tall and golden brown, with a dark streak down the center of his nose. His big dark eyes locked on Naomi, and she said, "He's beautiful."

"He is," Toby agreed. "I've had Legend with me since I was a kid. He's been living out at Mom's ranch, but I brought him here to Paradise a couple months ago. He's old, and I wanted him to live out the rest of his life here. With me."

"He doesn't look old." She reached out one hand to stroke the horse, but Toby grabbed her hand and pulled her back. "What's wrong?"

"Probably nothing. You just have to be careful around him. Like I said, he's an old man now and pretty damn crotchety." Toby held the horse's bridle tightly so she could slide her hand across the big animal's neck. "He gets so he doesn't like anybody— even me," he said, with a chuckle. "So I just want you to be cautious with him."

"Oh, you're not dangerous, are you?" Naomi was no stranger to horses. It would be impossible to grow up in Royal, Texas, and not be at least comfortable around them. She'd never had her own horse and hadn't really ridden much since high school, but she'd always liked them. And Legend, she could see, meant a lot to Toby.

"You just like getting your own way, don't you?"

she cooed as she stroked and petted the horse. "Well, I do, too, so we'll get along fine, won't we?"

"You the horse whisperer now?" Toby asked.

She shot him a look from the corner of her eye. "He's male, isn't he? A woman always knows her way around a crabby man."

"Is that right?" One corner of his mouth tipped up.

God, he smelled good. He shouldn't smell good after standing out in the early-morning sun, sweat already pearling on his chest and back.

"I've talked you out of every bad mood you've ever had."

He laughed again and stroked Legend's nose. "Not much of a test, since I'm not a moody guy."

"Oh, really?" She tucked her arm through the handle of the basket and looked up at him. "When you couldn't get the hydraulic lift to work on the patio table you built to go below ground?" It had been a terrific invention and one of her favorites that he'd come up with.

A picnic table that seemed to dissolve into a patio, with the push of a button, it lifted, pieces sliding into place until it was a concrete-topped table big enough to seat six. When you wanted it, there it was. When you didn't need it, it disappeared, leaving only a patio behind.

"That was different," he said, a slight frown on his face.

"How?"

"That wasn't moody. That was frustration."

"Frustration *is* a mood," she pointed out, pushing her hair back from her face. "But did I talk you out of it or not?"

That frown slid into a smile of remembrance. "You did. Took me to the roadhouse for a beer and karaoke."

"You're a terrible singer."

"But I make up for it with enthusiasm."

Naomi laughed and felt everything in her settle. This was good. Hormones aside, this was what she needed, wanted. This easy affection. They were friends, and they always would be. She'd see to that.

"Okay," she said, giving Legend one last pat, "now that I've won an argument—"

"Not an argument. No one shouted."

"A debate, then," she amended. "I have chickens to assault and eggs to kidnap. If you don't hear from me in half an hour, come and find me."

"You're taking this whole rancher's wife thing to heart, aren't you?" he asked, and his mouth was still curved in a smile.

"If I'm living here, I'm doing my share of chores," she said. "As long as the chickens don't kill me." She looked past him to the horse. "Legend, it was nice meeting you. Toby, I'll see you at breakfast."

She headed for the corral gate and stopped when Toby laughed. Turning around, she saw that Legend had pulled free of Toby's grip to follow her. "I've never seen him do that before," he admitted.

"I'm new here, that's all," she said and kept walking. But now she heard the horse's hooves plopping onto the powder-soft dirt right behind her. Naomi stopped again and this time waited for the horse to come close. Staring up into those chocolate-brown eyes, she smiled and said, "You're on my side, aren't you?"

The horse lifted his huge head then laid it gently on her shoulder as if giving her a hug. Touched, Naomi whispered to the big animal and stroked his neck as she would have a puppy.

She looked over at Toby and saw amazement on his face as he watched her. And Naomi thought that maybe this was all going to work out, after all.

Six

The next couple of weeks were harder than Toby had thought they would be. Living with Naomi was both torture and pleasure.

She was his friend, but more and more, he was noticing her breasts, her butt, her smile, her low, full-throated laugh that tugged at something deep inside him. Lust, pure and simple, he told himself. Now that she'd relaxed about her pregnancy and he'd gotten her to loosen up and actually eat real food, she was curvier than ever, and that was giving him some bad moments.

He didn't want to feel for her. Didn't want to start feeling a need for more. But he didn't seem to have a choice in that. Cursing under his breath, Toby grabbed a screwdriver, stepped behind his latest project in the workshop and tightened the screws there. He smoothed his thumb over them to make sure they were deep set, then took a long walk around the piece, inspecting every inch before moving to test the design. Better to keep busy, he told himself. To keep his brain so full of work it didn't have time to pick apart thoughts of Naomi.

The workshop was his sanctuary. When Toby had the ranch built, he'd had this shop done to his specifications. The floor was hardwood, as it was easier to stand on for hours than concrete. The windows were wide enough to let in plenty of natural light, plus there were skylights in the roof. The walls were peppered with sketches he'd stuck there with pieces of tape. There were walls full of shelves holding every kind of supply he might need. And the wall behind his bench was covered in Peg-Board so he could hang his favorite tools within easy reach.

On the far side of the building, he had lumber, plastic, metal and vinyl and a table saw to let him cut anything down to whatever size he needed. This building was the one spot in the universe that was all his. No one came in here, so he was always guaranteed peace and quiet and the solitude he needed to spark ideas. He'd come up with some of his best stuff in this shop, and whenever he was here, his brain kicked into gear.

Until lately.

"Just keep focused." He studied the raw version of his design, looking for areas he could improve. If it worked as it was supposed to, of course, he'd redo the whole thing in finer materials and, with patent in hand, get it onto the market. It was what he did, what he'd been doing most of his life. Taking ideas and making them real. A few of those inventions had helped him amass a fortune that had allowed him to buy this ranch and live exactly the way he wanted to.

"And nothing's going to change just because Naomi's here," he muttered. But hell, even he didn't believe that. Things had already changed.

Having Naomi around constantly was like having an itch he couldn't scratch. He hadn't counted on that. Her scent was everywhere. It was like she was stalking him. In his sleep, in the kitchen, hell, even here in his workshop he couldn't get her out of his mind. She'd invaded every part of his life, and what was worse, he'd *invited* her in. He'd done this to himself by coming up with that marriage-of-convenience idea. Now his skin felt too tight, his mind was constantly filled with images of her and she was looking at him as she always had. As good ol' Toby.

"And that's how you've got to stay," he said tightly. Once he got used to her constant presence, he'd get over the whole want-to-strip-her-naked thing and their relationship would smooth out again. That would be best. He didn't want any more from her than friendship, because anything beyond that was too damn risky. He could deal with the sexual frustration. But if she got any deeper under his skin,

Toby could be in trouble. And he'd had enough female trouble to last him a lifetime already.

So he deliberately pushed everything but the moment at hand out of his head. All he needed was to keep his distance from her once in a while. Clear his head. Get some space. Like today. Some time spent in the workshop, focused on what he loved doing.

"Toby," Naomi called, walking into the workshop. "You in here?"

"So much for that idea," he muttered. "Yeah." He raised his voice. "In the back."

Sanctuary was gone now, so he braced himself for being near her. It was just as well she was sleeping in the stupid guest room, he thought. He didn't know if he could take it, having her in his bed every night and *not* touching her.

He heard her footsteps and could have sworn he smelled her perfume rushing toward him. Toby didn't dare take a deep breath to steady himself—he'd only draw more of her into him. And he was already on the slippery edge of control.

"Wow, you've been busy," she was saying as she got closer.

He turned to watch her as she approached and asked himself how any man could keep his mind on work when Naomi Price was around. Hell, she was his friend, and right now it felt like a damned shame to admit it.

Shaking his head at his own disturbing thought, he turned back to the shelf unit.

"I've got a few more projects hitting the market in the next couple months," he said.

"Like what?"

One thing he gave Naomi, she'd always been interested in his inventions. Wanting to know what they did, how they worked and how he'd come up with them.

"There's a self-leveling measuring cup—" He glanced at her as she came closer. "My mom loves to bake and complains that there are different kinds of cups. For dry or liquid. This cup does both and levels itself so you know you're always right."

She gave him a smile, and it lit up her eyes. Toby looked away fast, but not fast enough. The pit of his stomach jittered, and a little lower, his body went rock hard. Damn it.

"Your mom'll be happy. What else?"

She picked up a wood dowel and twirled it in her fingers. Those long, slender fingers with the deep red polish on the nails. He looked away again.

"Something Scarlett wanted," he said and made a minor tweak to the hydraulic system. Anything to keep his brain focused. "She keeps her vet tools in the trunk of her car and had one of those flimsy trunk organizers. The one I designed is heavy acrylic, with a hinged lid and compartments that slide out with a button push." He checked the mechanism on the back of the piece again. "I figure it'll be a hit with carpenters, plumbers, artists, even fishermen. They'll be able to keep their stuff handy and safe."

"Wow." She dropped the dowel onto the workbench. "Okay. Made your mom and Scarlett—not to mention millions of others—happy. What've you got for me?"

He looked at her in time to see a wide smile flash across her face. *What did he have for her?* Well, now, that was a loaded question, wasn't it? Rather than face it, he asked, "What do you need?"

She propped one hip against the workbench, threw her amazing long copper-streaked brown hair back behind her shoulders and said, "Surprise me."

Damn. Everything she said now tempted him, and he knew she hadn't meant it that way. "I'll do that."

"So, what're you working on now?"

"This? It's a prototype for a new piece of furniture," he said, relieved to shift his thoughts back to safe territory. He stood back, folded his arms over his chest and said, "Look at it. Tell me what you see."

Frowning a little, she moved to get a better look. Sadly, she moved closer to him, and her scent wrapped itself around him.

After a second or two, she shrugged. "It looks like a bookcase. At least the top half does. The bottom half looks like it's a cabinet door, but you don't have any pulls on it yet."

He grinned. "Don't need them. See that switch on the side there? Give it a turn."

She did, and the machinery inside hummed into life. Naomi moved out of the way and watched, a smile on her face, as the cabinet door swung out and

up until it was horizontal, jutting out from the bookcase itself. "Cool. It converts to a table."

"There's more," Toby said and, stepping forward,
reached under the table and pushed another switch
to one side. Instantly, hidden benches lowered from
beneath the table and took their places, one on each
side.

She laughed. "I love it. Table and chairs in a bookcase."

He liked that approving smile and took a seat on
one of the benches as he waved her toward the other
one. "In a small place? Buy this bookcase, and you
have a table when you want one and it's gone when
you don't."

She propped her elbows on the table and rested
her chin on her joined hands. "For a man with a gigantic house, you're really into space-saving mode,
aren't you?"

He ran his hand over the table surface. "I like
coming up with things that can be multifunctional."

"It's brilliant. I love it." She looked at the top half.
"And the bookcase stays in place so you don't have
to unload it before using the table. Very cool."

"Thanks." He looked at the piece again. "There
are some products like this on the market, but none
that include benches along with the table and none
that use hydraulics like I'm using them."

"Another patent for the boy inventor."

"Haven't been a boy inventor for a long time," he
said, shifting his gaze back to hers.

FREE Merchandise is 'in the Cards' for you!

Dear Reader,

We're giving away FREE MERCHANDISE!

Seriously, we'd like to reward you for reading this novel by giving you **FREE MERCHANDISE** worth over **$20** retail. And no purchase is necessary!

You see the Jack of Hearts sticker above? Paste that sticker in the box on the Free Merchandise Voucher inside. Return the Voucher today... and we'll send you Free Merchandise!

Thanks again for reading one of our novels—and enjoy your Free Merchandise with our compliments!

Pam Powers

Pam Powers

P.S. Look inside to see what Free Merchandise is **"in the cards"** for you!

We'd like to send you two free books like the one you are enjoying now. Your two books have a combined cover price of over $10 retail, but they are yours to keep absolutely FREE! We'll even send you 2 wonderful surprise gifts. You can't lose!

REMEMBER: Your Free Merchandise, consisting of **2 Free Books** and **2 Free Gifts**, is worth over $20 retail! No purchase is necessary, so please send for your Free Merchandise today.

YOUR FREE MERCHANDISE INCLUDES...
2 FREE Books **AND** 2 FREE Mystery Gifts

FREE MERCHANDISE VOUCHER

2 FREE BOOKS and 2 FREE GIFTS

Please send my Free Merchandise, consisting of
2 Free Books and **2 Free Mystery Gifts**.
I understand that I am under no obligation to buy
anything, as explained on the back of this card.

225/326 HDL GLTD

Please Print

FIRST NAME

LAST NAME

ADDRESS

APT.#   CITY

STATE/PROV.   ZIP/POSTAL CODE

NO PURCHASE NECESSARY!

HD-517-FM17

For one long, humming second, the air between them nearly bristled. Toby stared into her eyes and wondered if she could read the hunger no doubt shining in his. She licked her lips, huffed out a breath and opened her mouth to speak. But whatever she might have said was lost, and the mood between them shattered, when another voice called from the doorway.

"Hey, you two! I'm on the clock here. No canoodling."

"Canoodling?" His eyebrows lifted. "Scarlett's here?"

Ruefully, Naomi smiled. "That's what I came to tell you. She's here to give Legend a checkup. I took him from the corral into his stall to make it easier on her. You know, out of the sun. It's really hot out there."

Toby shook his head again. "You mean you walked to the stall and he followed you."

"Pretty much. What can I say? He finds me irresistible."

A lot of that going around, Toby thought grimly. His horse loved her, and Toby couldn't stop thinking about her. Naomi Price was making life on the ranch a hell of a lot more interesting than he would have believed.

"Hello? You coming out or do I have to come in?" Scarlett's shout was tinged with laughter.

"We're coming!" Naomi called back and got up. She headed for the front door, then stopped and looked back at Toby.

Through the skylight, sunlight poured down over her like a river of gold. It highlighted the copper streaks in her brown hair and made her brown eyes glow like aged whiskey. Her body was curvier than he'd ever seen it, and the rounded mound of the baby made her seem softer, more alluring than he wanted to admit. She stood there, watching him, the hint of a smile on her face, and everything in Toby tightened into a hot fist.

"You coming?" she asked.

"Nearly," he muttered, and stood up slowly, trying to mask the signs of his body's reaction to her. "Yeah. Be right there."

As soon as he could walk again.

A few days later, Naomi had her files—folders with clippings and printouts of websites she was interested in—scattered across the dining room table. The room, just like every other one in the house, was perfect. At least to Naomi. The table was a live edge oak, long enough to seat twelve and following the natural contours of the tree it had been made from. The grain was golden and gleaming from countless layers of varnish and polish. A fireplace along the wall was unlit, and in the cold hearth were ivory candles on intricate wrought-iron stands. The windows across from Naomi gave her a view of the paddock and the fields stretching out beyond.

Naomi had the whole house to herself, since Toby was at Clay Everett's and Rebecca was in Royal doing some grocery shopping. Funny, Naomi used to be alone so much of the time she had convinced herself she loved it. Now that she lived with Toby and had the ranch hands popping in and out and Rebecca to sit and talk to, the house today seemed way too...*quiet* with everyone gone. On the other hand, she told herself, she could get some of her own work done with no interruptions.

With her new plans for the show, Naomi wanted to line up guests who could come in and demonstrate different ideas. And she knew just where she wanted to start. There was a place in Houston that specialized in faux stone finishes. It was owned and operated by a woman who'd started her business out of her garage. The show would be good for Naomi and good for the woman's company.

She shuffled through a pile of papers looking for the number, and when her cell phone rang she answered without even looking at caller ID. "Hello?"

"Ms. Price?"

"Yes." Frowning slightly at the unfamiliar voice, she said, "If this is about a survey or something, I'm really not interested—"

"I'm calling from Chasen Productions in Hollywood."

Naomi swallowed hard and leaned back in her chair. Panic, curiosity and downright fear nibbled at her. Hollywood? She took a breath, steadied her voice and said calmly, "I see. What can I help you with?"

"My name is Tamara Stiles, and I think we can help each other."

"How so?" *Wow.* She silently congratulated herself on sounding so calm, so controlled, when her insides were jumping and her mind was shrieking. Hollywood. Calling *her.*

"I've seen your show, and I'd like to talk to you about perhaps taking it national."

Naomi lurched up from her chair and started walking, pacing crazily around the long table. This couldn't be happening. Could it? Really? Her show. On national TV?

"National?" Did her voice just squeak? She didn't want to squeak. Oh, God, she couldn't seem to catch her breath and she really wanted to sound professional.

"That's the idea," Tamara answered. "Do you think you could come to Hollywood next week? I'd like to meet in person to see what the two of us can come up with."

Clapping one hand to the base of her throat, Naomi said, "Um, sure. I mean, yes. Of course. That would be great. I'd love to meet with you." *Understatement of the century.*

"Fine, then. Give me your email and I'll send you my contact information. I can arrange for your flight and hotel—"

"Not necessary," Naomi said, instantly wanting to stand on her own two feet. Sure, it would be nice if a Hollywood producer paid for her travel, but if

Naomi did it herself, *she* remained in charge. They exchanged information, and then Naomi said, "I'll email you when I have particulars."

"Excellent. If you could be in town Monday, that would work well for us here."

"Monday is doable." Even if it wasn't, she'd find a way to make it work. Hollywood? Taking her show national?

People had enjoyed her local cable show, and it was getting more popular, but Naomi knew that her parents considered it more a hobby than anything else. This would convince them that she was so much more than they thought.

There were too many emotions crowding around inside her. Too many wheeling thoughts and dreams of possibilities. She was starting to shake, so she got off the phone as quickly as possible. There was no one there to tell. She needed to tell Toby, but she couldn't do it over the phone.

So Naomi just sat there in the silence. Alone. Smiling.

Later that night, Toby listened and watched as Naomi paced back and forth in the great room. She hadn't stopped talking since he got home, and honestly, he couldn't blame her. Pretty big deal getting a call out of the blue from Hollywood. Good thing the great room was as big as it was, though. Gave her plenty of space to walk off her nerves.

"Can you imagine?" she asked. "Hollywood? Calling me?"

"Well, why wouldn't they?" Toby said from his position on the couch. He was slouched low, feet crossed at the ankles, hands folded on top of his belly. "Even California's got to hear about it when a show takes off like yours has."

She stopped, threw him a grin that was damn near blinding. "You have to say that. You're my best friend."

There it was. Best friend. No lust. No need. Just pals. As it should be. If only his brain would get the memo. "You're great at what you do, Naomi. Half of Texas is talking about you, and the other half will be soon. Why not Hollywood?"

"You're right. Why not?" She started pacing again, her steps getting quicker and quicker as her words tumbled over each other. "Tamara," Naomi said, "isn't that an elegant name? Very showbizzy."

"Showbizzy?"

She shot him another wide smile. "I'm rambling and I know it. Heck, I can hear myself babbling and I can't seem to stop. Until you got home, I was talking Rebecca's ears off. She was too nice to tell me to be quiet and go away."

"Maybe she's pleased for you," he pointed out.

"She is. I know. But you're the one I wanted to tell, Toby." Naomi stopped dead, looked at him from across the room and said, "It about killed me waiting for you to get back from Clay's, because I just couldn't tell you this over the phone."

"Next time you need me," he said, sitting up, leaning his forearms across his knees, "call. I'll come home."

"Okay. Thanks. I will." She took a deep breath, laid one hand on her rounded belly and sighed. "Toby, this is just so crazy. Am I crazy?"

"Not that I've ever noticed."

"I've got to get tickets. And a hotel reservation."

"For both of us," he said, and she looked at him in surprise. Didn't she know that he would stand with her? Didn't she realize that Toby knew what this meant to her? That everything she'd been working toward for the last few years was finally coming true?

"Really? You'd come with me?"

"I'm not going to let you go alone." He shifted on the couch and dropped one arm along the back. "Naomi, I get it. This show, it's who you are. And someone noticing, wanting to talk to you about making it even bigger? I know what it means to you, so no, you're not going alone."

"You really are the best, Toby," she said, her voice soft, almost lost.

He shook his head, smiling wryly. "Who'll you talk to while you pace a hole through your hotel room floor?"

At that, she stopped pacing, darted across the room and dropped onto the chocolate-brown leather couch beside him, curling her feet up beneath her.

She was so close he could see the excitement glittering in her eyes. Feel the warmth radiating from her and the scent of her, drawing him in again.

Laying one hand on his forearm, she admitted, "It was so surreal. Hollywood wants *my* show, Toby. It's a dream. And okay, maybe nothing will come of it, after all, and I'm completely prepared for that, but it's a *chance*. It tells me people are noticing."

"I know." He covered her hand with his.

"You know," she went on, "when Maverick first started all his trouble, I thought for sure the world was ending, and now look at me. I'm marrying my best friend and going to Hollywood to talk about my show."

Best friend. He took a breath and let it slide from his lungs. No matter what else happened, he would remain her friend, and that would be easier, he told himself, if he let go of her hand and slid just a bit farther away from her.

"Oh!" Her eyes went wide, and her mouth dropped open.

Instant panic clutched at his throat. "What? What is it? Is it the baby? Are you okay?"

She didn't answer him, just kept looking at him through wide eyes shining with something far more magical than the promise of Hollywood. Then she took their joined hands and laid them on her belly. "It moved. The baby moved, Toby."

His insides settled now that he knew she was okay. But then the baby moved again, the slightest ripple of movement beneath his hand, and he felt the magic still glittering in her eyes. "That was…"

"I know," she said breathlessly. "Wait for it."

She pressed his hand to her belly, and Toby held his breath, hoping to feel that rustle again, and when it came, they smiled at each other. Secrets shared and a moment of real wonder connected them more deeply than ever before.

"Isn't it amazing?" Naomi launched herself at him, planting a hard, fast kiss on his mouth that changed instantly from celebration to something else entirely.

Heat erupted between them, surprising them both. Toby's heart jolted into a fast gallop, and Naomi did a slow melt against him, parting her lips under his. His tongue swept in, tangling with hers, tightening the knots inside him until he was pretty sure they'd never come undone. His hands fisted at her back. Her hands stroked his shoulders and slid up into his hair, her fingers holding him tightly to her. Seconds passed, and the building heat between them became an inferno.

Toby had never felt anything like it, and he wondered how he'd been so close to her for so many years and never tried this. She moved against him, sliding onto his lap, and he knew she felt the hard proof of what he was feeling for her, because she squirmed on his lap, making it both better and worse all at the same time.

When that thought hit, Toby knew he had to end

this. Before they completely crossed the line they'd agreed on to protect them both. He broke the kiss, lifted her off his lap and set her down on the couch. Then he got up, needing some space between them.

"Toby—"

He looked over his shoulder at her and nearly groaned. Her mouth was full and tempting, her eyes wide with surprise and her breath coming in short, hard gasps. He knew the feel of her, the soft curves, the warmth and eager response to his touch. And damned if he knew how he'd ignore that knowledge now.

"Just give me a minute here, Naomi," he ground out and pushed both hands through his hair. He dragged in a deep breath and shook his head.

"Why did you stop?" she asked.

Toby spun around and glared at her. "You're kidding, right?"

"No." She pushed herself off the couch and walked toward him.

Toby held up one hand to keep her at bay. Her hair was loose on her shoulders. The T-shirt she wore clung to her rounded belly, and her white shorts displayed way too much tanned leg. Her bare feet didn't make a sound on the floor, but it was as if every step thundered in his head, his chest, as a warning. Well, he was going to listen.

He'd been burned once by a woman he cared too much for, and he wasn't going to set himself up for that again. They were going to be friends. Nothing more.

"Toby, that was—"

"A mistake," he finished for her and walked to the bar in the far corner of the room. Yanking the mini fridge open, he pulled out a beer, opened it, then slammed the fridge closed again. He took a long pull of the cold, frothy brew and hoped to hell it served to put out the fire burning inside him. Somehow he doubted a beer was up to that task, though.

"Why does it have to be a mistake?" she asked. "We're engaged, aren't we?"

"Yeah," he said, taking another drink. "And it's a marriage of convenience, remember? We agreed to no sex. It'll just complicate everything, and you know it."

She scowled at him. "Nobody said anything about sex tonight, Toby. I'm talking about a kiss."

"A kiss like that?" He waved one hand at the couch where they'd been just moments ago. "Leads one place, Naomi."

"Wow. You're really sure either of yourself or of me." She tipped her head to one side to watch him like he was a bug on a glass slide. "You think kissing my brains out means I'm just going to leap into your bed shrieking, 'Take me, baby'?"

"I didn't say that."

"You didn't have to." She pushed that silky mass of copper-brown hair back from her face. The better to scowl at him, he guessed. "For God's sake, Toby, I'm not that easy."

He snorted, shook his head and took another gulp of his beer. "You are many things, Naomi, but I never thought *easy* was one of 'em."

"Right." She folded her arms across her middle, unconsciously lifting her breasts so that the tops peeked out of her T-shirt's neckline. "But you figured one hot kiss from you and I was going to toss my panties over my head?"

"You're twisting this up somehow," he said and tried to figure out exactly where he'd taken the wrong tack.

"Oh, I don't think so." She walked toward him, and as short as she was, she looked pretty damn intimidating when she had a mad on.

She stopped about five feet from him and said, "I liked kissing you—which, okay, surprised me a little—"

He snorted again and nodded. It had surprised the hell out of him, too. Hell, his mouth was still burning.

"—that doesn't mean I'm ready for more, though. But we are engaged, Toby." She wagged a finger at him. "You're the one who's waking me up at six in the morning so Rebecca won't find out we're not sleeping together."

"Yeah, so?" He frowned a little, not following her train of thought.

"Well, don't you think she'd expect to see an engaged couple kissing now and then?" she asked, sarcasm dripping from her tone. "Hugging? Looking like we're intimate even if we're not?"

He hadn't considered that, but she had a point. If he kept treating her like a pal or a little sister or something, Rebecca would notice and start wondering. "Damn it."

"Ah," she said, satisfied. "Good. Now maybe you won't freak out over a simple kiss. And you'd better get used to the idea, because we should do more of it."

Insulted, he countered, "A, I didn't freak out. B, there was nothing simple about that kiss."

"You don't think so?" she asked, turning around and heading toward the door. "For me, it was nice, but nothing special."

He stared after her, stunned. She was playing him. Had to be. Because that kiss had nearly lifted the top of his head off, and he'd damn well *felt* her heart beating a wild rhythm. No way was she as unmoved and blasé about it as she was pretending.

When she was at the door, she paused and looked back at him. "Seriously, Toby, if we're going to make Rebecca and everyone else believe this marriage is real, then we'd better practice kissing until we're good at it."

She gave him a half smile and left. Toby stared

at the empty doorway for a long count of ten, then tipped his beer back for another drink.

"Practice? If we get any better at it, I'm a dead man."

Seven

Dinner at the TCC on Saturday night was a treat. Naomi had always liked the club, and once women were allowed in as members, she'd taken full advantage of her new rights. She, Cecelia and Simone had headed the redecorating committee, and they'd done what they could to spruce up the old place.

Not that they'd been given free rein. But painting the entryway and the restaurant and the ladies' room had helped to brighten things up. They were too steeped in tradition here to willingly let go of the Texas artifacts, documents and pictures decorating the walls, and a part of Naomi understood it. She was a Texan, too, after all. But at least those walls were painted a soft gray now, with fresh white trim, and it looked brighter in here even with the dim lighting.

Sitting across the table from Toby, she took a second to admire it. The dining room in the Texas Cattleman's Club really hadn't changed much in decades, and even with a fresh coat of paint, it remained very much what it always had been—an upscale restaurant with roots in the past. Tables were draped in white cloth, and on every table was a bud vase with a single yellow rose in it. Soft jazz spilled out of overhead speakers, and the brass sconces on the wall threw out shafts of pale light. The atmosphere was old-world, but the clientele was a mixture of the older generation and younger. Conversations rose and fell like the tides, with a sprinkling of laughter now and then to keep things bright.

Naomi looked at Toby and just managed to squelch a sigh. He wore a white dress shirt, black jacket and black slacks. His black boots were shined to perfection, and he'd capped everything off with a black Stetson that made him look like a well-dressed outlaw. Her insides shivered, and her stomach did a long, slow roll. That sensation still caught her by surprise, despite how often she'd been experiencing it lately.

Desire pumped through her and she fought it down, because really, he hadn't said a word about that kiss since it happened two nights ago, so maybe he hadn't felt what she had. Wanted what she had—did.

And maybe she'd been trying to tempt him, to remind him of that kiss when she chose what to wear tonight. Her short, bright red dress hugged her breasts and her growing curves proudly. The neckline was square and deep and supported by inch-wide straps across her shoulders. Her red heels gave her an extra three inches of height, which she was always in favor of—plus, they made her legs look great.

He'd noticed, because she'd seen the flare of approval in his eyes when he first saw her tonight. But he'd been cool, controlled, even a little distant since they sat down at the restaurant.

Two days since she'd kissed him on impulse and found so much more than she'd expected. When his mouth fused to hers and his arms came around her, every cell in Naomi's body had come alive. Sitting on his lap, she'd felt his body tighten, and just remembering it now had her shifting slightly in her seat.

But long, luscious kisses couldn't make up for the sheer panic in his eyes when he pulled away from her. When he'd announced that for her own good, he was stepping back.

Infuriating to think about it even now. Naomi made up her own mind, and she didn't appreciate him making decisions for her. After all, she wasn't the type to just leap into bed without thinking about it. Although, she thought as she glanced down at her baby bump, she'd done it at least once. And maybe that was what Toby had been thinking. That she'd slept with Gio so easily, why wouldn't she jump *him*, too?

God, that was humiliating.

Especially when it was true. If he'd made the slightest move, Naomi would have willingly gone to bed with him, and forget the bargain they'd made. She'd never felt anything like that kiss before, and oh, how she wanted to know what else he could make her feel.

"What in the hell are you thinking about?" he asked, his voice a low rumble.

"What?" She jolted a little, immensely grateful he couldn't read minds.

"Just a tip, Naomi, but poker's not your game." He shook his head. "I'm sitting here watching your expression shift and change with every thought running through your brain. Want to tell me what's going on?"

"Nothing," she said. Though she wanted to talk about that kiss *and* the way he'd pulled back and shut her down, this wasn't the place for that conversation. Not when they were surrounded by half the town. "I'm just mentally packing, preparing for the trip tomorrow."

"Right." Clearly, he didn't believe her. But he was going to accept it. "Okay. Wes said he'd have his jet ready to leave whenever we get to the airport."

Toby had arranged to borrow Wes Jackson's private jet for the trip to LA, and Naomi was looking forward to it. She was so nervous about this upcoming meeting that being able to pace restlessly on the flight was going to be nice.

Actually, Toby had taken not only their flight but

their hotel reservations out of her hands and didn't mention it until it was done. She should have been irritated, since she was completely capable of making reservations, but instead, she thought it was sweet. Which only went to prove that their kiss had seriously short-circuited her brain.

"You didn't have to ask Wes for the use of his plane."

Toby shrugged. "He wasn't using it. Said it was no big deal, and it's better than flying commercial."

"It would have to be," she said and tried a smile. His eyes gleamed in the candlelight as he watched her. "I'm glad you're still going with me."

"Why wouldn't I?"

"After the other night…" There, she'd brought it up anyway, despite vowing that she wouldn't. But then again, it was hard *not* to talk about something that was constantly on her mind.

"You were right," he said, tapping his fingers against the tabletop.

"That's unexpected," she said, keeping her voice even, soft, not sure where he was going with this. "But I'm always happy to hear it. What was I right about?"

He leaned closer. "About showing affection for each other. If we want to make this marriage look real to everyone, then you were right." As if to prove it, he reached across the table and took her hand in his.

Heat skittered up her arm to settle in her chest.

His thumb stroked the back of her hand, and his gaze locked on hers. "I'm with you, Naomi. For the long haul. We made a deal, and I keep my word. You know that."

"I never doubted it," she said honestly. No matter what else, Toby McKittrick kept his promises. Which meant, she thought sadly, that he would not be the one to cross that no-sex line. If the line was to break, it was up to her to do it. Now all she had to do was figure out if it was what she really wanted or not.

"Good. So we'll show affection. Make this marriage as real as we can..." He paused, then added, "While keeping to the bargain we already made." As if everything were settled, he gave her hand a pat and let her go to sit back and pick up his after-dinner coffee.

Naomi stewed quietly. How was it possible to both win and lose at the same time?

"Naomi!" Cecelia, a wide smile lighting up her face, hurried up to their table with Deacon just a few steps behind her. "Oh, I'm so glad we ran into you tonight." She glanced across the table. "Hi, Toby. Don't mean to interrupt, but I just have to tell someone."

"What's going on?" Naomi asked, standing to hug her friend.

Cecelia gave her a squeeze, then reached back for Deacon's hand before looking at Naomi again. "We just found out today. We're having a girl." Her eyes filled with tears that she blinked furiously to keep at bay. "God, I've been tearing up all afternoon. Can't seem to stop myself. Don't really want to. I'm going to have a daughter, Naomi."

Happy for her friend, Naomi pulled her in for another hug and then kissed Deacon's cheek. "Congratulations, you two."

"Yeah," Toby said, "add mine to that." He shook Deacon's hand. "That's great news. Really."

"Yeah, it is," Deacon said, pulling Cecelia to his side and holding on to her as if worried she might try to make a break for it. "And if she's half as gorgeous as her mother, she's going to be a beauty."

"Deacon…" Cecelia sighed a little and went up on her toes to give him a kiss. "When will you find out, Naomi? Can't wait to see what you're going to have."

"I was thinking about being surprised," Naomi admitted, only because she couldn't say that up until a couple of weeks ago, she hadn't really allowed herself to think about the baby.

"Oh, how will you get things ready?" Cecelia asked. "No, you've got to know. The suspense would kill me."

Laughing, Naomi said, "I'll think about it."

"Okay, good. Now, we're going to have dinner and plan our baby girl's future, right up through college," Cecelia said, laughing. "Oh, Naomi, you can help me with the design and furnishings for the nursery…"

"I'd love to." It would be great practice for setting up a nursery at the ranch. She hadn't even begun to think of that, but that was not surprising, since there'd been so much more to concentrate on lately.

"Okay, we'll talk soon."

When Cecelia and Deacon walked off to their own table, Naomi sat down again and watched Toby as he reached for the check folder.

Cecelia was in love and lucky enough to have Deacon love her back. Naomi shot a sidelong glance at Toby as he tucked several bills into the folder for their waiter. He loved her, she knew. But he wasn't *in* love with her, and that was the difference between her relationship and her friend's. Still, Naomi was lucky, too. Toby was here. With her. He'd changed his life around to be there for her.

And they'd had that kiss that had stirred up feelings she'd never suspected she had for him. Was there something more than friendship between them? Was it worth the risk of losing him to find out?

Los Angeles was big and noisy and crowded, and Naomi loved it. From the packed freeways to the mobs of tourists wandering down Hollywood Boulevard, everything was so different from what she knew that Naomi felt energized. Of course, being with Toby had that effect on her, too.

From flying on Wes Jackson's private jet to their penthouse suite at the Chateau Marmont in West Hollywood, it was as if she and Toby were wrapped up in some fantasy together. The two-bedroom suite was decorated in pale grays, with hardwood floors, beamed ceilings and glass tables. There was a tiled terrace off the living room and a waist-high concrete balcony railing. The gas fireplace in the main room flickered with dancing flames, because though it was June, it was also Southern California. The damp air coming in off the ocean meant the fire was welcome as well as beautiful.

Naomi spent that first night alone in her bedroom, unable to sleep—not just because she was nervous about her meeting with the producer the following morning. But because Toby was right there with her and still so far away.

He'd been as good as his word, making small, affectionate gestures in front of Rebecca and the hands who worked for him. But when they were alone, he was careful to be...*careful*. He didn't seem to be having any difficulties keeping his distance from her. So maybe she was wrong about all this, she told herself. Maybe she was the only one who couldn't stop thinking about that kiss. Who couldn't help wondering what more might be like.

"How'd the meeting go?" Toby sat across from her, a sea breeze ruffling his hair as he watched her, waiting. He'd loosened the dark red tie at his neck and left off his steel-gray suit jacket. The long sleeves of his white dress shirt were rolled back to the elbows, and his long legs were stretched out, crossed at the ankle. Toby was probably the only man she knew who could pull off black cowboy boots in Los Angeles.

They were on the terrace of the penthouse suite, and evening was settling in. On the glass-topped table between them was a pitcher of iced tea and two tall glasses provided by room service. It had been a long day. Naomi'd had her meeting with the producer, and Toby had taken care of some business with his patent attorneys. This was really the first chance they'd had to talk since breakfast in the restaurant that morning.

Naomi took a breath and sighed it out. How did she explain what it had been like to hear Tamara Stiles praising *Fashion Sense*? All her life, she'd been striving to matter. Maybe it had started out as an effort to finally earn her parents' pride, but at some point her motivation had shifted. It wasn't only about them anymore, but about Naomi herself. She'd wanted to prove to everyone—including herself—that she was more than a rich man's daughter. That she had more to offer.

Okay, a cable television show about fashion wasn't curing cancer or ending nuclear war, but she *was* helping people, she told herself silently. Giving them ideas on how to improve not only their looks, but their lives. Looking your best meant that you *felt* your best. Sure, she enjoyed what she did, but knowing that other people did, too, was what made it all so good.

Now, here in Hollywood, she'd reached the very thing she'd been aiming for. There were people here who wanted to produce her, make the show bigger, get a larger audience, really help Naomi be *heard*. And she wasn't thrilled. She should be. This was the pot of gold at the end of her own personal rainbow. This was the X marks the spot on her private treasure map.

Looking at Toby, she tried to tell him what she was feeling, but she couldn't explain it, since she wasn't sure herself yet. Maybe she just needed time to think. Distance to put it all in perspective.

"Naomi?" His features reflected concern. "It didn't go well?"

"No," she answered quickly with a shake of her head. "It went fine. She loves the show—said it has great potential."

He frowned a little at that. "Potential? What's that supposed to mean? It's already a hit in Texas. Hell, it's why she wanted you to come talk to her."

"Thanks. That's what I thought, too." Naomi tried to settle and couldn't, so she stood up and walked the length of the private terrace. He was right when he'd once said she needed room to pace when she was thinking. But this time, she felt as though she could walk all the way back to Texas and things still wouldn't be clear.

When she came back up to the table, she didn't look at Toby, but instead turned to face the valley view, her hands flat atop the wide concrete rail. "Tamara says for the show to go national we'd naturally have to make changes. To the sets, the kind of shows we do, pretty much everything."

"If she loves it, why does she want to change it?"

She looked over her shoulder at him. "Funny, I asked myself that same question."

"You should." He stood up, too, and joined her at the railing.

A sea breeze drifted through Hollywood and brushed past them like a damp caress. Naomi pushed her hair back and lifted her face into that soft wind before looking up at Toby.

He was so steady. So strong. And she was so grateful he'd come with her. She was out of her element here. In Royal, even in Houston, she was fairly well-known. But here she was just one of a crowd of supplicants trying to take that next step up on a Hollywood ladder.

Resting one hip against the balcony rail, she said, "Tamara says the show had something on its own— and that the Maverick video and all the hype that happened after on social media really gave it the kind of push they need to bring up a local show."

"Okay…"

"But," she said, shifting her gaze again, out to the valley and the smudge of ocean she could see in the distance, "to go national, the show has to be polished, have less of a small-town feel, so that it will appeal to everyone."

"Small town?" he asked. "Houston, Dallas— they've signed on already. They're not exactly small town, and it works for them just as it is."

"It does," she said, and again, Toby was saying pretty much what she'd said to herself after leaving the meeting. "She says that with a bigger studio and professional crew—not to mention scriptwriters—we *might* make it big."

"Might."

"Well, she can't guarantee it, of course," Naomi admitted. "And I wouldn't have believed her if she'd tried. But I never saw a problem with our studio in Royal."

"Seems to work fine," he agreed.

"And the crew are very professional. Even the interns from the college know what they're doing." She'd already made these arguments to Tamara. Gone over them time and time again by herself after the meeting, too. But it didn't change anything.

"They do."

"She said," Naomi added after a long minute, "that at first, they'd want to do the taping here. In Hollywood."

He went still. "So you'd have to live here."

"That was part of it, yes." She looked at him again and tried to read what he was thinking. But except for the flash in his eyes, his features were cool, blank. "They would, in theory, tape a short season all at once, so I'd have to be here in California for at least a few weeks."

"Weeks." He nodded thoughtfully but didn't say anything else.

Seconds ticked past into minutes, and still the quiet between them grew. Naomi's own mind was racing, going over the meeting again, what living in

California for weeks at a time might mean to her. To Toby. The baby. There were too many questions and too few answers.

"This is Hollywood, Toby," she said a little wistfully. "They're the experts. And this chance, it's what I've been aiming for."

"Sounds like you got it." No inflection to his voice, giving no clue to what he was thinking.

"I don't know," she said softly. What was more, she didn't know if she wanted it anymore.

Yes, LA was exciting. Hollywood had such cachet, deserved or not. Even their hotel, the Chateau Marmont, was a legend in a town filled with them. Movie stars as far back as the '20s had stayed in this hotel, and it was as if their spirits remained, because the hotel felt...out of time somehow. The stars still flocked here—movie stars, TV actors, singers all flocked to this place, this city.

Dreams were born, lived...or died, all in this one city.

And Naomi didn't know anymore if she wanted what was offered here. "This all comes back to Maverick's video," she mused, shaking her head at the irony of having something she hated be at the base of what could be the realization of her dreams.

"Well," she amended, "I guess it was more about how we handled the video than the video itself. That's what caught her attention, really. Tamara said she liked how we turned it around, used that video to spark more changes on the show..."

"Not we, Naomi," Toby said softly. "*You*. You did it. You faced Maverick down, took that ugly video of his and made it work for you."

She smiled to herself and pulled a lock of wind-blown hair from across her eyes. "You know, I really did. But, Toby, without you I don't think I could have. You're the one who helped me see that hiding wasn't the answer. You were right there. Standing with me. Helping me. You gave my baby a father."

His eyes darkened, swirled with emotions that flashed past too quickly for her to read. And suddenly, she didn't care what he was thinking, feeling. Right now all she knew was what *she* felt.

"Ever since we kissed," she said softly, sliding her hand along the railing until she found his and covered it with her own. "I've been thinking about more."

"Me too." He looked down at their joined hands, then into her eyes.

"That no-sex line you talked about?" she said, despite the tightness in her throat, the galloping of her heart. "The one you said we shouldn't cross?"

"Yeah?" His eyes darkened again. A muscle in his jaw twitched.

"I want to cross it."

"Me too." Toby reached for her, and she went to him eagerly. He pulled her in close, locked his arms around her and kissed her with a raging hunger that shattered every last thread of control she might have clung to.

Naomi lifted her arms to hook around his neck

and held him to her as his mouth took hers. Their
tongues tangled together in a silent dance of passion
that sent tingles of expectation skittering through her
veins. Better even than the kiss that had filled her
dreams for days, this one promised more than just a
few minutes of heat. This kiss promised an inferno
to come, and Naomi readily jumped into the flames.

She lost herself in the wonder of the moment, of
having him touch her, hold her, kiss her. For days
she'd been hoping to feel this again. For days she'd
watched him try to keep a safe distance between
them. And now at last, the wall separating them was
coming down in a rush.

His hands swept up and down her back, and
Naomi wanted to peel out of her sleeveless sunshine-
yellow dress. She wanted his hands on her skin—
those strong, rough hands that showed such gentle-
ness. She wanted all of him against her, inside her.

He tore his mouth from hers, and for one horrible
second, Naomi thought he was going to pull away
from her again. To back off from what was happening. Breath catching in her lungs, heart pounding in
her chest, she looked up at him and knew she needn't
have worried.

"That's it," he muttered thickly and bent to scoop
her up into his arms.

"Toby!"

"Quiet," he ground out through clenched teeth.
"We're too far gone to stop now, Naomi. I swear

I will stop, though, if you say no," he added. "So don't say no."

She shook her head, cupped his cheek in the palm of her hand. "I'm not. I'm saying hurry up."

"That's my girl."

Eight

He marched through the living area and straight into the big bedroom. There were two in the penthouse suite, and last night they'd been in those separate rooms. Not tonight, though, Naomi thought. Tonight, things would change. He walked to the wide bed, reached down and tugged the silky gray duvet off and let it slide to the floor. Then he set Naomi on her feet but kept a firm grip on her as if half-afraid she'd disappear if he stopped touching her. But she wasn't going anywhere.

Naomi turned in his grasp, pulled her hair to one side and said softly, "Help me with the zipper?"

He did, his fingertips trailing along her spine as the material fell open. She shivered when he bent to kiss the base of her neck, and an instant later, her dress was sliding off her body to lie on the floor like a puddle of sunlight. Wearing just her cream-colored bra and panties and a pair of three-inch taupe heels, she stood in front of him, letting him look his fill.

She was a little nervous, because her body was so different now. Naomi had been so careful for so long, counting every calorie, watching every bite, but since Toby's proposal, he'd been coaxing her to eat more. Now Naomi was rounder, fuller, and the mound of the baby was distinct enough that she actually thought to cover it with her hands.

He stopped her, though, holding her hands in his and tugging them aside. "No, don't hide from me." Shaking his head, he let his gaze sweep over her, top to toe and back again. A slow smile curved his mouth. "You make a hell of a picture, Naomi."

What she saw in his eyes made her feel beautiful. Desirable. She released a breath she hadn't known she was holding and reached for the buttons of his shirt. Then she pulled the tie from around his neck and tossed it onto a nearby chair. "You're wearing too many clothes," she whispered.

"Yeah, we can take care of that." He did. In what felt like a blink, he was undressed, laying her back on the bed and covering her with his body.

She sighed at the first contact of skin to skin. God, it felt good. Right. The cool sheets at her back, Toby's hot skin against the front of her. Sensations swarmed inside her, and she fought to breathe past the rush of them.

She smoothed her palms across the broad expanse of his chest, and he hissed in a breath in reaction. Naomi smiled, loving how much he was affected by her. Knowing that he was as swept away as she was. She rubbed her thumbs across his flat nipples until he groaned deeply, then dipped his head to take one of her hard nipples into his mouth.

Her smile slipped away, lost in the rising tide of heat enveloping her. His tongue swirled across her sensitive skin, and he ran the edge of his teeth across her nipple as well. Naomi moaned softly and arched her back, moving into him. When he suckled at her, she whispered his name, threaded her fingers through his hair and held him to her.

She didn't ever want him to stop. Naomi's eyes closed on a wave of heat swamping her senses. She'd never known anything like this before. The feel of his mouth on her was incredible, and when he ran one hand down the length of her body, she shivered. His hands, so scarred and callused from years of hard work, touched her skin with a rough tenderness that left her breathless.

He lifted his head, and she nearly whimpered at the loss of his mouth against her breast. But she stared up into his eyes and felt herself falling into that churning aqua sea of sensations. How had she gone so long, never knowing what they could create together? Never knowing what it felt like to have his hands on her skin?

"I've wanted this for a while now, Naomi," he

whispered, stroking one hand across her breasts, down her rib cage. "But you've gotta be sure."

She actually laughed a little, to think that he was giving *her* a way out this time. But no, they were through turning from each other. For tonight, for now, all that was important was the two of them. She didn't even want to think about tomorrow, but there was one thing she had to reassure herself on.

"I'm absolutely sure. But, Toby—" She paused and took his face between her palms. "Remember what we promised each other. No matter what else happens, we stay friends."

"Honey, right now I'm feeling *real* friendly." He grinned, took her mouth in a long kiss that had her insides melting into a puddle, then said, "Yeah. Friends. Always."

She nodded, because she was too full of emotions to speak. Naomi couldn't even identify everything she was feeling. All she knew was that in this moment in time, she was right where she wanted to be. But neither of them needed words right now. All they needed was to *feel*. To explore. Experience.

As if he heard her thoughts, he slid one hand down her body to stop over the curve of the baby she carried. Naomi went perfectly still, wondering what he would do, what he was thinking. Pregnant women couldn't be very alluring, right?

"Stop thinking," he ordered in a hush.

"What?"

"You're worrying. About how you look, of all

things." Toby shook his head as his gaze met hers. "Can't you tell that I think you're the most beautiful thing I've ever seen?"

"Toby—"

He smoothed his hand across her baby bump, then bent to kiss both her and the child within. There was so much tenderness in the action, in his eyes, that in that instant, Naomi was lost. Her heart filled to bursting, she felt the sting of tears in her eyes and impatiently brushed them away. She wanted nothing to blur this image of him. Instead, she etched it into her heart and mind so she'd never forget.

He looked up at her, his eyes shining, and all she could think was that she loved him. Beyond friendship, beyond sense, beyond anything. Naomi was in love with Toby. With her best friend.

When had it happened? Had it always been inside her, just waiting to be recognized? And what was she supposed to do about this realization now? If Toby knew what she was feeling, he'd pull away again, and Naomi knew she wouldn't be able to stand that. So she'd hide what she felt. Keep it locked up inside her so she wouldn't have the pain of seeing him turn from her.

Reaching for him, she stroked her fingers over Toby's cheek, then across his lips, defining them with the lightest of touches. There was so much she wanted to say to him and couldn't.

Finally, though, when she was sure her voice

wouldn't break, she said only, "You're going to make me cry."

"Oh, no," he assured her, giving her a slow smile and a wicked wink. "I'm going to make you scream."

"Promises, promises," she said, keeping it light, not wanting him to guess at what she'd just discovered.

"I always keep my word," he reminded her, then shifted his hand down to cup her center.

Naomi gasped and instinctively lifted her hips, rocking into his touch, wanting more, *needing* more. And he gave it to her. His thumb caressed that one sensitive spot while he speared two fingers into her heat. Within and without, Naomi felt on fire. She wouldn't have been surprised to see actual flames licking at the mattress beneath her.

She grabbed at his shoulders, her fingers flexing to hold on as gentle exploration gave way to desperation.

He kissed her, touched her, lavished attention on Naomi's breasts, her neck, her inner thighs, driving her wild with a kind of need she'd never known before. She'd never thought of herself as particularly sexual, but right now her body was pleading for release and the only man who could give it to her was bent on drawing out the torture of expectation.

"You smell so damn good," Toby whispered against her throat. "Your scent stays with me everywhere I go." He kissed her neck, licking, tasting. "You're there in my sleep, Naomi. I can't shake you."

"Then stop trying to," she told him, and he lifted his head to look at her.

"Yeah," he said, "I'm done with that. You're here to stay."

One breathless second passed, then two before he kissed her, taking her mouth in a celebration of need and passion. God, she wanted to drink him in, drown in him and what he was making her feel. She couldn't touch him enough. Hair, face, shoulders, back. She loved the feel of his muscles shifting beneath her palms.

Then he moved to kneel in front of her, and Naomi held her breath as he entered her. One long, slow thrust and he claimed everything she was, and she sighed as a shiver slid through her body. Lifting her legs, she wrapped them around him and pulled him deeper, higher.

His body moved in hers, in a rhythm that moved faster and faster. She groaned, sighed, at the luscious feel of his hard length taking her so completely. Silently, he offered her more, demanded the same. He looked down into her eyes, and she couldn't have looked away from that heated stare if it meant her life.

Anticipation coiled in the pit of her stomach as tension settled even deeper within. Naomi moved with him, racing to match his rhythm, rushing toward whatever was waiting for her. Always before, sex had been a quick bout of stress release. A subtle pop of pleasure that had left her mildly satisfied and silently wondering what all the big fuss was about.

Then she found out. His fingertips stroked her core while his body moved in hers, and she shattered, clawing at his back, whimpering his name through a throat so tight air could barely pass. Mind spinning, she held on to him and rode the pulsing flashes of brightness that seemed to blind her.

"Toby!" Her hips were still rocking with the force of that climax, and before she had time to adjust, to understand, he was pushing her past that pleasure to a place she'd never been before.

Her body felt raw, too sensitive, too *everything*, but Toby was relentless. "I can't," she whispered, shaking her head, looking up at him. "I mean, I already—"

"Again," he said tightly and drove himself deep inside her. He lifted her hips, tossed her legs over his shoulder and went even deeper than he had been.

Naomi wouldn't have thought it possible, but while her body was still quivering from the most amazing climax she'd experienced, she felt it preparing for another. She could barely breathe and didn't care. Her head tipped back into the mattress as her hands reached for his thighs. She was lifted so high she had no way to match his movements. She was at his mercy, and he was showing none.

Naomi had never been so at the mercy of her own body. She'd never known the kind of overwhelming sensations that were taking her over. Had never been so out of control with a man. Never let any man take her over as Toby was doing. And she hadn't even guessed that her body could feel so much.

He was unstoppable. Indefatigable. His hips were like pistons, pumping into her, pushing her past all boundaries, all restrictions. Naomi stared up at him, licked her lips and knew that nothing would ever be the same again. Not after this. Not after Toby.

"Come on, Naomi," he whispered, voice low. "Let me watch you fly. Let go, Naomi. Just let go."

"I am, Toby," she said breathlessly, as her heels dug into his back. He was battering away the last of her defenses. Tension clawed at her. That first orgasm was as good as forgotten in her body's rush to claim another.

"Now, Naomi," he whispered, his big hands holding her bottom, squeezing soft flesh, giving her one more sensation to add to the mix. "Come now."

She laughed a little, but the sound came out as a sob for air. Her hands slapped at the sheets, clutching the fabric as if looking for a way to hold herself in place. "You're not giving me a choice. I feel—"

"Look at me," he said, and she heard the fight for control in his voice.

She opened her eyes, met his, and while their gazes were locked, he pushed her over the edge of desire into a completion that was so foreign to her that she was lost in the sweeping tide of it. Naomi stared into those aqua eyes as her world rocked and her body splintered. She screamed, unable to stop the wild rush of release as it grabbed her and shook her down to the bone.

Naomi watched him, lost in those eyes, as her body, still trembling, held on to his and cradled him as he let himself go.

When he collapsed on top of her, Naomi held him tightly. Their hearts raced in tandem, their bodies quaking as if they were shipwrecked survivors clinging to each other for safety. But it was so much more than that.

He rolled to one side, taking her with him, and Naomi laid her head on his chest, listening to the steadying beat of his heart. Loving him was going to be hard, she knew, but there was nothing she could do about it. He was in her heart forever. And she would never, for as long as she lived, forget what they'd shared here tonight. On the night she knew she loved him.

Toby lay there like a dead man. If the hotel had been on fire, he'd burn to a crisp because there was no way he could move. He doubted his legs still worked.

Hell, he'd been with plenty of women in his time, but not once had he experienced anything like what had just happened between him and Naomi. He scraped one hand across his face and stared at the ceiling. He'd crossed a line. Hell, he'd *erased* the line. And he didn't give a good damn. All he could think about was that he wanted her. Again. Now.

She curled on her side and slid one leg across his, and the silky glide of her skin against his stirred him into need in a flat second. Who knew that there would be such heat between them? He rubbed one hand down her back, and she cuddled into him, sliding her palm across his chest. She was…amazing. More than that, but he didn't have the words. What he had was need that only she could meet.

That was dangerous territory, though, and he had to lay out some signposts before they headed farther down this road. Now that the line was gone, new ones had to be drawn. To protect both of them.

"Toby…"

She whispered his name on a breathy sigh, and instantly his body tightened. Didn't seem to matter that he barely had his breath back from the most incredible sex of his life—his body was apparently raring to go again.

But right now he had to give his brain the upper hand. If he could manage it while she was looking at him through soft eyes, her tongue running across her bottom lip. *Oh, man.*

"Okay, we need to talk," he said and winced because he'd just sounded like a damn cliché.

"No, we don't," she said and smoothed her fingertips across his nipple.

"That's not helping." Muffling a groan, Toby caught her hand in his and held her still. If she kept touching him like that, talking would be the last thing on his mind. "Naomi, this changes things."

She chuckled, tipped her head back and looked up at him. "It sure does."

"Not funny," he warned, going up on one elbow and rolling her over onto her back. Still, seeing the softness and the humor in her eyes, he nearly smiled back. Then he remembered the line. Smoothing her hair back from her face, he ran his fingers through the long, silky threads and had to fight to concentrate. "We have to talk about what this is going to mean between us."

She sighed, stiffened a little, then said, "That it'll be even easier for us to show affection toward each other?"

Oh, he wanted to show her some affection right now. But before anything else got started, he had to make sure she knew there was a limit on how much he was willing to give. How much he was willing to risk.

He looked into her eyes—eyes that shone like warm whiskey—and shook his head. Taking a deep breath to center himself, he said, "Sure. Yeah. That's a good point. But what I want to say is…" Hell. What *was* he trying to say?

Naomi pushed herself up slightly, bracing one hand against his chest. "Want me to say it for you? That I shouldn't let my little heart fall in love with you because you're not interested in love?"

"Naomi…"

"Or is it that you don't want me to make the mistake of thinking that our marriage is going to be real all of a sudden?"

"That's not what I was going to say," he argued, though he had to admit it was pretty damn close.

"Right." She tipped her head to one side. "You can stop panicking, Toby. We were friends and now we're friends plus. That's all. I get it. That about sum everything up?"

Sounded like it did. Although why it bothered him that she was being so reasonable about it all, he didn't know. He hadn't expected calm, and he should be grateful for it. Toby wasn't even sure why he felt oddly...disappointed. "Yeah, I guess it does. Look, the point is, we had the no-sex agreement, and that's shot to hell—"

"Not going to say I'm sorry about that," she put in.

"No, me either," he admitted. They could at least be honest with each other. "But I have to make sure you know that sex doesn't mean—"

She pushed herself off his chest into a sitting position, shoved her tangled hair back and looked him dead in the eye. "For heaven's sake, Toby. I'm not going to throw my heart at your feet. I know you, remember? I know that Sasha messed your head up so bad you don't even want to hear the word *love*."

His frown deepened. Was it a blessing or a curse that Naomi knew him so well? "This isn't about Sasha," he ground out.

"Oh, please. It's always about Sasha. That miserable excuse for a woman was never right for you, and," she said, lifting one eyebrow meaningfully, "if you'll remember, I told you that at the time."

"Yeah. I remember." His expression soured. "Thanks for the *I told you so*."

"No problem." She scooted off the bed, stalked to the window and stared out at the deepening twilight.

The growing darkness seeped into the room as well, shadows filling every corner. Toby's gaze followed the line of Naomi's back and down to the curve of her behind. The woman had a great behind. Then, when she turned to look back at him, she was profiled and her breasts were high and full, the rounded outline of the baby on full display. She was beautiful. Even the fire in her eye couldn't dim his reaction to the woman.

Then she started talking. "Sasha leaving was the best thing to happen to you."

He gritted his teeth. "This isn't about Sasha."

"It's all about her," Naomi continued. "Has been since the day she walked out with her pretty-boy country singer. She's gone, Toby, but you're still caught up in that drama."

He sat up and leaned against the headboard, the sheet pooling at his hips. "What the hell are you talking about?"

"You." Naomi walked back to the side of the bed and glared down at him. "She's moved on, Toby, but you're still running your life by what happened to you with her."

"No, I'm not."

"Really? You haven't been involved in a single relationship since she left." She crossed her arms beneath her breasts. "Why?"

"Not interested."

"Liar." Now she frowned at him. "At least be honest and admit that you won't let yourself trust anyone anymore."

"I trust you," he pointed out. And why did he suddenly feel as though he had to defend himself?

She sighed as if disappointed, but damned if he knew what the problem was.

"Toby, you're cheating yourself out of maybe finding something amazing, all because Sasha convinced you that feelings weren't to be trusted." She bent down and tapped her index finger against his chest. "Well, you're wrong to give her so much power."

"How did this get to be about Sasha?" he asked, shoving himself off the bed to stare down at her. "She doesn't run my life. Never has. Never will. I stopped thinking about her the day she left Royal. I live my life the way I want to, Naomi."

"You're probably the most stubborn man I've ever met."

"Thanks."

"Not really a compliment." She sighed a little and chewed at her bottom lip.

He dropped both hands to her hips and pulled her in closer. She had to tip her head back to meet his eyes, but she did. "I trust *you*. That's good enough for me."

"Okay," she said, nodding, watching his eyes. "I just don't want you to be sorry one day for marrying me and cheating yourself out of love somewhere down the line."

"We're getting married, Naomi." He smiled softly. "And hell, if we get sex, too, all the better."

Her returning smile wasn't wide, but it was there. "Yeah, that works for me, too."

"I do love you, Naomi. Always will. I just don't want you to think of what we have as more than what we have."

"Got it. You're not in love with me."

"Right." He didn't know what the hell he was feeling at the moment, but it wasn't the kind of love that people built dreams around. He knew that much.

"Fine. Don't worry about it." She shook her hair back and said, "Oh, stop looking like you're kicking a puppy. I'm a big girl, Toby. I walked into this with eyes wide open, and I didn't ask for undying declarations of romantic love."

No, she hadn't, he realized. In fact, she was acting like what had happened between them was no big deal. And he didn't know how he felt about that. Damn it, Naomi had a way of turning everything around on him so that Toby didn't know whether he was coming or going, and she'd just managed it again. Was he worried about nothing?

"So, are we finished talking?" she asked, running one hand down his chest, across his abdomen and lower still, to curl her fingers around the thick, hard length of him.

He hissed in a breath through his teeth. "Yeah, I think that about covers everything."

"Good to hear," she said and kissed him while her fingers moved on him, sliding, caressing. "So don't just stand there, cowboy. Show me what you've got."

"Challenge accepted," he muttered. He felt like he was going to explode. How could he want her so desperately? Lifting her, he half turned and braced her back against the closest wall. "Not slow this time, Naomi. This time it's gonna be hot and fast."

She leaned into him, wrapped her legs around his waist and nibbled at his neck. "Show me."

Hard and aching, he slid inside her and instantly felt her body tighten around his. Silky heat surrounded him, and he groaned as Naomi scraped her nails across his skin and hooked her ankles behind his back. She met him eagerly, hungrily, and his brain short-circuited as he stared into the eyes of a woman he'd thought he knew.

Her body, his, moving together, in a mad, wild tangle of desire and need that gripped them both. One corner of his mind yelled at him to lay her down, take his time with her. But that calm, reasonable voice was shouted down by the other half of him demanding that he have her. Now.

"Toby, Toby..." She twisted her hips on him, increasing the friction, increasing the need until he thought he'd go blind with it.

"Come on, baby." He kissed her, hard and long and deep, and took her breath as his own, devouring her as she was devouring his body. "Come with me. Come with me now."

He felt her body tighten, felt the first flickering pulse of her climax and watched her eyes glaze. And while she rocked with the orgasm shaking through her, he forgot about control and emptied himself inside her.

Caught in the web spinning between them, Toby knew that in spite of what he'd said before, nothing would ever be the same.

Nine

After a few days in LA, Naomi was ready to be home in Texas. Now that she was back home, she might miss Hollywood a little, but it was good to be back. As summer heated up and June inched toward July, the days got longer and the people moved slower. It was an easier pace than the big city, and that was part of its appeal. She'd heard people say that anyone could live up north, but it took real character to make it through a southern summer.

Naomi wasn't so sure about that. But one thing she did know—she was grateful the Royal Diner had AC. The minute she and Toby's sister, Scarlett, stepped inside, Naomi almost whimpered.

"Oh, it's going to be one ugly summer," Scarlett said as she signaled to Amanda and then tugged Naomi to a booth.

Naomi flopped onto the red vinyl bench seat and stacked her shopping bags beside her. "I let you talk me into buying too much."

"It's never too much," Scarlett said. "Besides, you're getting married. You need…stuff."

Stuff didn't begin to describe all the things Naomi had picked up that morning. She and Scarlett had spent the last several hours at the Courtyard Shops, a great collection of eclectic shops where you could find anything from antiques and crafts to fresh local produce. But there was also a new bridal shop owned by Natalie Valentine.

And *that* shop was where Scarlett had pushed Naomi into going a little nuts. She was only carrying a few of the things she'd bought. The rest were being delivered to the ranch. Naomi wanted a small wedding, in the evening, maybe, out at the ranch. She hadn't talked to Toby about it yet, and she knew her mother wouldn't be happy with the venue, but Naomi was. A small, simple wedding, with just their families and friends there, made the most sense to Naomi. After all, it wasn't as if this was ever going to be a *real* marriage.

Her heart ached at that thought, but she had to acknowledge the truth, no matter how painful. Toby was never going to know she loved him. Never going to love her back. And she had to find a way to be all right with that. If she couldn't…then maybe marriage wasn't the answer. For either of them.

"I love the dress you picked out," Scarlett said. "That pale yellow just looks gorgeous on you, and knee length will keep you from passing out in this heat."

"Thanks," Naomi said. "I like it, too. My mother will no doubt want me in yards of lace and tulle, but that doesn't make sense for a backyard ceremony. And besides," she added wryly, "it's tacky to wear white on your wedding day when your baby bump is showing."

Scarlett laughed a little, then shook her head. "You're going to be a beautiful bride. But are you really sure you want it held outside? Even in the evening it'll be hot."

"I'm sure," Naomi said. "We can have the reception by the pool, and if it gets too hot, people can go into the house for a break. Of course, I haven't talked to Toby about any of this yet, so he may have different ideas…"

Scarlett waved one hand at her. "He'll be good with whatever you want. He loves you, right?"

Sighing a little, Naomi leaned toward the other woman and whispered, "Scarlett, you know the truth. I know Toby told you."

"Sure, I know," she said. "And I know my brother. He's a great guy, Naomi, but he's not going to marry someone just to do her a favor. He cares for you. I can see it."

Care was a long way from love. Too long. Since they got back from California, they'd shared a bed and shared each other, every night, every morning and one memorable afternoon in the workshop. But they hadn't talked about Hollywood. Hadn't talked about their wedding. Hadn't talked about anything important. It was as if they were both holding back, and Naomi didn't know what to do about it.

"Hey, Naomi, you okay?"

"What?" Sighing, she shook her head. "Sorry. I drifted."

"To somewhere nice? Maybe cooler?" Scarlett asked.

"No, stayed right here in Royal. Scarlett, can I ask you something?"

"Sure."

"Are you good with this?" Naomi asked. "I mean, me and Toby getting married. You're okay about it?"

"Absolutely." Scarlett paused when Amanda Battle walked up to their table. She slid two tall glasses of ice water onto the table, and Scarlett sighed. "Bless you, my child."

"Thanks, I'll take it," Amanda said, laughing. "You two been running around buying out Royal's shops?"

"Just put a dent in a few of them," Naomi assured her. Her stomach rumbled, reminding her of why they'd come to the diner. And a salad just didn't sound the least bit appetizing. "Can I get a turkey sandwich? Potato salad?"

"Oh, me too, please," Scarlett said.

Amanda nodded and hurried off to tend to other customers. So when they were alone again, Scarlett took a long drink of her water, then said, "Anyway, why wouldn't I want you married to Toby? You're way better for him than Sasha was."

"Low bar there, but thanks," Naomi said drily.

"What's going on?" Scarlett watched her for a long minute. "You don't seem as excited as I thought you'd be over everything. I mean, you're engaged, pregnant and have Hollywood knocking on your door."

"It's complicated," Naomi said and thought that might be the understatement of the century. She still didn't know what she was going to do about the offer from Tamara Stiles, and she had to let them know soon.

But if she took it, she would be giving up the kind of control that had made the show *hers* in the first place. And did she really want to live in Hollywood for weeks at a time? If she did, what about Toby? Would he move there with her? Stay on the ranch? And what about when she had the baby? What then? Would she be dragging the baby from state to state?

"Wow. Judging by your expression, wish I could buy you a beer."

Naomi sighed. "Me too. Or the most gigantic glass of wine in the state of Texas." She took a long drink of her ice water, letting it soothe her dry throat. "There's just so much going on right now, and I'm still getting emails from people about that stupid video—"

"No one who knows you cares about that thing, Naomi," Scarlett said.

"I know, but millions of people who don't know me have seen it." Just thinking of that made her want to cringe. Didn't matter if she'd managed to turn the tables on Maverick. That she'd taken his vicious attack and made it work *for* her.

Whoever Maverick was had tried to ruin her life, and knowing that person was still out there made her nervous. He'd wanted to make her life a misery. Wouldn't it infuriate him to realize that he'd inadvertently helped Naomi rather than hurt her? Wasn't it likely that he'd try something else in order to make trouble for her?

"Okay, yeah," Scarlett allowed, "millions of people saw the video, but now they're tuning in to your show, so hey. Win for you." She picked up her water glass, waited for Naomi to do the same and then clinked them together in a toast. "Seriously, don't let that weirdo bother you. I'm sure Sheriff Battle's going to find out who Maverick is and stop him. Soon."

"I hope so," Naomi confessed. "I can't help wondering if he's going to be frustrated at how the video worked for me and try something else."

"I understand why you'd be worried about that, but honestly, I don't see it happening." Thoughtful,

Scarlett looked at her. "Why would he? There're still plenty of people in Royal to screw with."

"Talking about Maverick?"

Both women looked up at Gabe Walsh. He was tall and gorgeous and his hazel eyes always held a gleam of humor. His dark blond hair was militarily short, and he had a lot of intricate tattoos. Formerly FBI, he now owned a private security firm based in Royal.

"Sorry," he said, mouth curving into an unrepentant smile. "Didn't mean to eavesdrop, but I heard you talking as I was walking to my table. Maverick the subject of interest?"

"Who else?" Scarlett asked.

"Everyone's talking about him," Naomi said. "Especially those of us he's already attacked."

Gabe winced. "Yeah, I get that. And I know the guy's caused a lot of misery around here. But I just left my uncle Dusty, and I swear all the intrigue and mystery surrounding this Maverick guy is really sparking my uncle's will to live. It's even making his cancer treatments easier for him to deal with."

Dale "Dusty" Walsh was in his sixties and used to be a big bear of a man. But Naomi had seen him not so long ago, and the chemo he was undergoing had whittled him down until he hardly looked like himself anymore.

"I'm glad to hear he's doing better," Naomi said, knowing nothing she said could make things easier on Dusty's family.

"I don't know about better," Gabe admitted sadly,

stuffing his hands into the pockets of his slacks. "But Maverick has sure perked Dusty up. The mystery of it has him intrigued and more interested than anything else has been able to do. I think he's trying to figure out who the guy really is."

"I hope he does," Naomi said with feeling. "I won't feel really safe until he's caught."

"He will be," Gabe assured her before he left to meet his friends for lunch. "No one can stay hidden forever."

Naomi wondered, though. For months, Maverick had proven elusive enough to avoid being caught. Who was to say anything would change? And if he came after her again…

Scarlett's cell phone rang, and when she glanced at the screen, she said, "It's Toby."

Naomi listened to the one-sided conversation, and when Scarlett hung up she asked, "What is it?"

"It's Toby's horse, Legend." All business now, she looked worried. "Toby says he's gone down and won't get up again. Sorry about lunch, but we have to get to the ranch." She waved a hand at Amanda and called, "We have to cancel. Sorry."

Naomi was already gathering her things, and when she pushed herself out of the booth, Scarlett was right behind her.

Toby hated feeling helpless.

Legend's labored breathing filled the air and brought Toby to his knees beside the failing horse.

Fresh straw littered the floor and rustled with every movement. Toby rubbed his hands up and down the big animal's neck. He felt each shuddering breath and the thready beat of Legend's big heart. Hell. He was old. The horse had had a long, great life. Toby had brought him to live with him at the ranch because he knew that Legend's life was coming to an end. And God, Toby wished he could do *something* to change what was happening.

He heard his sister's approach before he saw her and recognized the quick, lighter steps of Naomi coming in with her. He'd hated to interrupt their day out together, but he didn't want Legend to suffer. He owed his old friend that much. And damn it, he'd wanted Naomi with him.

Scarlett came into the stall with her doctor's bag and instantly went to work. Toby stood up, making room, and walked to where Naomi stood at the open door. She didn't say a word, just wrapped her arms around his waist and nestled her head against his chest. Toby held on to her like a lifeline in a churning sea and felt everything inside him settle.

Holding Naomi, he watched his sister examine the horse, and as he looked at Legend, he saw his own life flash in pictures through his mind. The day Legend arrived at Toby's home. The first time they rode off together, down back roads and out through the fields. He could still feel the excitement of being astride Legend and pretending to be everything from a great explorer to a Western outlaw. Life had been easy and full of possibilities, and Legend had been with him through all of it.

That horse had been the most important thing to him for a lot of years, and now it was time to let him go. Toby didn't need the sympathy shining in his sister's eyes to know Legend had run out of time. His heart ached with the truth.

"I can put him down gently, Toby," Scarlett said. "He'll just go to sleep."

"Oh, God…" Naomi's voice was a whisper, but he heard the pain in it and was grateful she was with him.

"Give us a minute with him first, okay?"

"Sure." Scarlett stood up, kissed her brother's cheek and said, "Call me when you're ready. I'll be right outside."

"Thank you." Naomi squeezed Scarlett's hand as the woman slipped out of the stall.

Toby walked to Legend's side and held out one hand to Naomi for her to join him. The horse's breathing was more labored, and his eyes wheeled as if he were trying to understand what was happening.

"Poor Legend," Naomi whispered, then bent to kiss the horse's forehead. "You're such a good boy. Such a good horse."

"He loves you," Toby said simply, watching as Legend tried and failed to rest his head in Naomi's lap.

She lifted tear-drenched eyes to Toby's. "I'm so sorry. So sorry you have to lose him."

"I know. I am, too." He stroked the horse's side, then back up to his neck and face. Bending down to look into the big brown eyes of his oldest friend, he said, "We had a great life together, Legend. And I'll never forget any of it."

The horse jerked his head as if agreeing, then tried to stand, failed and fell back into the straw again. It broke Toby's heart to watch the valiant old horse try so desperately to stand and be what he once was.

"Easy, boy," he said quietly. "It's all right. You can go on now."

Naomi never stopped stroking him, whispering to him as the horse labored on until Toby couldn't stand it any longer. Glancing at Naomi, he saw her tears and felt his own. But it did none of them any good to drag this out. Best to say goodbye and let Legend go on to the next adventure.

"Scarlett?"

"I'm here." She stepped into the stall, sympathy etched into her features.

"Do it," Toby said. "But I'm staying with him."

"*We're* staying with him," Naomi said, gaze locked with his.

"Yeah. We." Toby nodded, his throat too full to speak.

"Not a problem," Scarlett said. "It won't take long and he won't suffer. I promise."

Toby tuned his sister out. He didn't want to think about it. Didn't want to watch her end the old guy's life, even though it was a blessing for Legend. Toby looked again into his horse's eyes, and he could have sworn he read a silent thank-you there.

Legend's breaths came slower, slower, then stopped, and the silence was almost unbearable. He was gone. A huge piece of Toby's life had just ended, and he felt like he'd been kicked in the gut. Naomi took his hand and held on. Scarlett kissed him again and silently left them alone.

"I'm so sorry," Naomi whispered, turning into him, wrapping her arms around him.

"I know," he said and held on to her, burying his face in the curve of her neck.

He'd wanted her there, with him, when he realized that Legend was dying. Toby had needed Naomi, and she'd come. Just as she always had. Her hand in his, he felt her warmth pouring into him and clung to it.

After the trip to California, things had definitely changed between Naomi and him. Sure, the sex was great. Amazing, even, but out of bed, he felt the strain between them. They hadn't talked again about the offer she'd had, and he had no clue what she was thinking. Planning. So he had to wonder what she was considering. Did she want that offer badly enough to leave Texas? Move to Hollywood? And if she did, what then? His life was here. In Royal. Living in California wasn't part of his game plan, but was it in Naomi's? That producer had offered a dream. Was she going to take it?

And if she wanted to, then maybe they shouldn't get married, after all. Was it fair to her?

That's bull, he told himself. All of it. He wasn't thinking about what was best for Naomi. It was about *him*. What he was feeling. Every time they had sex, he felt himself sliding farther down a steep cliff. Pretty damn soon, he'd find himself loving a woman and risking everything he'd promised himself he never would again.

Straightening up, he looked into those whiskey-gold eyes and knew he was in trouble. He just didn't know how to avoid getting in deeper. "Thanks, Naomi. For being here."

"I'll always be here, Toby."

He hoped so, but there was some serious doubt. Toby caught her cheek in the palm of his hand and realized that Naomi was really the only woman outside his immediate family whom he trusted completely. Why, then, was he so cautious about letting his feelings for her grow? Was it himself he didn't trust? Or was he just too damned cowardly to risk loving again?

Either way, he didn't come off too well.

Standing up, he drew her to her feet and said, "Come on. I have to get out of here."

"Okay." She held his hand and followed him out of the stall, where they both stopped and looked down at Legend one more time.

Then, together, they left the stable, and the pain, behind.

Ten

Two days later, Naomi was furious.

The text she'd received an hour before ran through her mind again.

Naomi, we must speak. Come to Oaks Hotel in Houston as soon as you can. Gio

The fact that he'd practically ordered her to come irritated her only half as much as the fact that she was going to see him at all. Why had Gio come to Texas? Why had he texted her out of the blue after making it perfectly clear he wasn't interested in her or her baby?

Temper spiked inside her. Naomi hadn't told Toby about Gio's text, because she knew he'd tell her not to go meet the man. But she had to, didn't she? Had to find out what he was up to. Why he was here. Had to tell him to go away and never come back. Once she had it all settled, she'd tell Toby about it, of course. She wasn't going to lie to him about this.

Over the past few weeks, Naomi had put Gio out of her mind completely. He had nothing to do with her or her baby. Toby was the man who would be her child's father. Toby was the man she loved. The man she was about to marry. Gio had no place in their lives. And the only reason she was going to see him was so she could tell him that to his face.

It was time to banish her past so she could go forward with her future.

She parked her car on the street, fed the meter and then hurried toward Gio's hotel. It was plush, of course, with a liveried doorman and a red carpet stretching from the sidewalk to the polished brass front door.

Naomi smoothed her palms over her cream-colored slacks, then tugged at the hem of her pale green blouse. The fabric was light but clung to the outline of her baby bump proudly. The doorman hurried to open the door for her, and she smiled at him as she stepped into the blessedly cool interior.

The spacious lobby was all wood, dark fabric and glass, giving the impression of old-world money and cool elegance. Naturally this was the kind of place Gio would stay. Looking around, she spotted the bar and headed for it. She was right on time for this meeting, and she didn't want to be here any longer than she absolutely had to.

The elegant bar held a luxurious hush. A long mahogany bar stretched along one side of the room, and a dozen or more small round tables dotted the gleaming wood-plank floor. Her gaze swept the room, and since there were only a handful of people in the room, she spotted Gio instantly. He had a table in the back, in a shadowed corner, and Naomi sighed. If he thought this was some kind of assignation, he was in for a disappointment. The only reason she'd agreed to meet him was that she wanted to look him in the eye and tell him to get lost.

Gio had been a blip in her life. A moment out of time in her past. He had no part in her future, and that was what she'd come to tell him. As she approached, her heels tapping on the floorboards, he noticed her, and Naomi stiffened in response. She still couldn't believe she'd been foolish enough to spend the night with the man, but in her defense, just look at him.

Not as tall as Toby, Gio had long jet-black hair, blue-green eyes and always just the right amount of beard scruff on his cheeks. He wore black slacks, a cream-colored silk shirt and looked, as always, very self-satisfied. The man was gorgeous, but he was as deep as a puddle.

"*Bella*," he crooned as he stood to meet her, "you are so beautiful."

"Thanks, Gio." She avoided the kiss he aimed

at her cheek and pretended not to notice his clearly false look of hurt and disappointment.

"Can I get you something to drink?" he asked, already signaling to the waitress.

"No, thanks."

He waved the waitress away again as Naomi took the seat opposite him at the small round table. She glanced around the room, making sure she didn't know anyone there, then focused on Gio again. Waiting.

"I'm so happy you came to meet me," he said and managed to look both pleased and disappointed.

"Gio," she said, "I don't know what this is about, but I'm only here to tell you I don't want anything from you—except," she added as she had a brain flash, "to have you sign away your parental rights to the baby."

"*Sì, sì,*" he said, waving his hand as if erasing the very thing she'd just asked for. "We will speak of all this. *After* we speak of something else..."

Okay, so it wasn't the baby he was interested in. No big surprise there, after the way he'd reacted when told he was going to be a father. So what had brought him all the way from Italy?

The room was quiet, and so was Gio's voice. He leaned toward her across the table, and Naomi had a moment to really look at him and wonder how she could ever have been attracted to the man in the first place. He was handsome, but in a stylized way that told her he spent a lot of time perfecting his look.

The just long enough hair, the right amount of scruff on his face, the elegant, yet seductive pose he assumed, half lounging in the chair. He couldn't have been more different from Toby.

Toby was a man comfortable enough with himself that he didn't need to set a scene so that a woman would admire him. All he had to do was walk into a room and his confidence, his easy strength, would draw every woman's eye.

No, there was no comparison between Gio and Toby. And now all she wanted to do was wrap this up and get back to the man she loved.

"The baby is growing, yes?"

Hard to miss that, she thought, since her top clung to the rounded curve of her belly. And as if the baby was listening, it gave her a solid kick, as if to say *Let's get out of here, Mom. Go home to Dad.* She smiled at the notion, and Gio smiled back, assuming her expression was meant for him.

Shaking her head a little, she said, "Yes. Everything's fine. And no, I don't need anything from you, Gio. I'm getting married, and *he* will be my baby's father."

Gio tapped one manicured finger against his bottom lip, then gave her a reluctant smile. "Yes, I have heard of your marriage plans." When she looked surprised at that, he shrugged. "Gossip flies across oceans, too, *bella*. You have the marriage with a very rich man. I wish you well."

Frowning now as a ribbon of suspicion twisted

through her, Naomi said, "What are you getting at, Gio?"

"Ah, so you are in a hurry. *Che peccato*—what a shame," he translated for her. "All right, then. I will sign your paper for you—"

"Good. Thanks."

"—*if*," he said, "you are willing to do something for me."

A cold chill swept along her spine, twining itself with the suspicion and quickly tangling into greasy knots that made Naomi shiver in response. Gio's eyes were fixed on hers, and she saw the speculative gleam shining in their depths.

"What do you want, Gio?"

"Ah. We will be businesslike, yes?" He smiled, and she saw briefly the man she'd slept with before he disappeared into a sly stranger. "*Bene*. We will be frank with each other. Is best."

"Then say it." She folded her hands together on the table in front of her and kept her gaze fixed on him.

"I will be quiet, *bella*, about being your bambino's daddy," he said with a wink, "*if* you agree to finance my next film."

She blinked at him. The one thing she hadn't expected to hear from him was a threat of blackmail. Gio was a filmmaker, but she knew his last two films hadn't done well. So apparently, he was having trouble getting backing. Enough trouble that he was willing to fly to America for the sole purpose of blackmailing *her*.

Naomi was so furious with him, with herself, she could hardly draw breath. But Gio was oblivious of her thoughts and feelings, and went on outlining his business plan.

"Since you told me about the bambino," he said, "I felt it my duty to check on you. And I have found that your fiancé is the man who invents so many wonderful things…" He gave her another of his *I'm so disappointed* looks and said, "He is very rich and yet you did not mention this to me. Why is that?"

"Because it's none of your business?" she ground out.

"But yes, it is." He leaned toward her again, reached out and covered her hand with his, and smiled into her eyes. "You will marry this man soon, yes?"

"Yes." One word, squeezed past the knot of fury and humiliation lodged in her throat.

"Then you are able to afford to help me, *si*? I have a film in production, and I want you to finance it for me. We will be business partners, *bella*!" He released her hand, sat back and smiled benevolently at her. "You, me, our bambino."

Blackmail. Plain and simple. It was an ugly word, but it was the only one that fit. Naomi felt like an idiot for ever involving herself with this sad, shallow man. She could only hope that her genes would wipe out whatever of Gio was lingering in her baby. But even as she thought it, she realized that Toby would be her child's father. He would be the role model her child needed—the guiding hand, the understanding heart—and that would more than make up for Gio's faulty genes.

"Do we have an agreement, *bella*?" He pursed his lips, shook back his hair and positioned himself in the single slice of light piercing through a window. "I will keep your secret about the baby. I will not demand my fatherly rights. All you must do is help me with this. Is not such a bad bargain, *si*?"

Naomi took a deep breath, shook her head and said, "No, Gio. It's not a bad bargain."

He smiled, clearly delighted with her.

"It's a terrible one."

His smile disappeared. "*Bella*, do not be foolish."

"You know when I was foolish, Gio?" she asked. "When I looked at you and saw more than was actually there. I'm thinking clearly now." Leaning across the table toward him, she said, "I won't give you a penny. You'll get nothing from me, Gio. Ever.

"So, you do your worst. Tell the world you're the baby's father. In fact," she said, as brilliance flashed in her mind, "I approve. Go ahead. Take out an ad in every paper…splash it across cyberspace, claim my baby as yours. It'll be easier to sue you for child support."

He gaped at her, his mouth opening and closing like a fish on a line. Oh, he hadn't expected this. He'd thought that Naomi would roll over and do just what he wanted to protect her own name. But she'd learned something with Toby's help. You stood up to bullies. You didn't let them dictate your actions. So she was taking a stand here, to protect herself *and* her baby.

He looked absolutely stunned, and the knowledge that she'd caught him off guard gave Naomi a huge rush of pleasure. Pushing up and away from the table, she looked down at him. "My husband will be my baby's father, and no child could ask for a better one. So do what you have to do, Gio. But you'll never get a dime from me."

Smiling, she turned around and stalked out of the plush bar. She felt...liberated, and she couldn't wait to get home to the ranch and tell Toby all about this meeting and how she'd handled it.

Naomi never noticed the man in the corner who'd been surreptitiously taking pictures during her encounter with Gio.

When his phone signaled an incoming text, Toby checked it, expecting to hear from Naomi that she was headed home from Houston. He opened it, stared and felt his stomach drop to his feet.

A picture of Naomi and a dark-haired man seated at a table together, looking cozy, as the man held her hand and looked meaningfully into her eyes. The message accompanying the photo was short and to the point.

You're a fool. She's meeting Gio Fabiani behind your back.

Gio. Her baby's father. Toby actually *saw* red. His vision blurred and darkened at the edges as he stared at the damning photo. Naomi was meeting the man who'd gotten her pregnant and turned his back on her. The man she'd claimed she didn't want anything to do with. Yet they looked pretty damn friendly, with him staring into her eyes while he held her hand.

She'd told Toby she was going to do some wedding shopping in the city. Instead, she'd gone to meet another man. She'd lied to him. So what else had she lied to him about? His heart felt as if it were being squeezed by a cold, tight fist. He couldn't breathe, because the cold rage rising inside was choking him.

This was exactly what he'd worried about. Getting closer to Naomi only set him up for the pain he'd felt the last time he allowed a woman into his life. Naomi knew what Sasha had put him through, and now she herself, the woman he'd thought of as his best friend, was doing the same thing?

Why was she meeting Gio? Was she playing both of them against each other? Was she planning on walking out on him in favor of the guy who'd gotten her pregnant?

"What the hell, Naomi? What the hell is going on?" He couldn't stop staring at the picture.

Maverick was behind this texted photo, he knew.

Who the hell else would be watching Naomi and making sure Toby knew what was happening? Bastard had a lot coming to him when he was finally caught.

Shutting his phone down, he stuffed it into his pocket as if he could wipe the image of Naomi with another man from his mind if he just didn't have to look at it. Pain stabbed at him. This was so much worse than when Sasha had walked out. It cut deeper because Naomi was a part of him. She'd been his friend. His lover. His fiancée.

And now she was…what? He didn't know. All he was sure of was that he had some thinking to do. He wouldn't hold her to their engagement if this Gio was what she really wanted. But he'd be damned if he'd wish her well with the guy. Betrayal stung hard and settled in the center of his chest.

"Damn it, Naomi," he muttered. "What the hell were you doing with him?"

After all they'd shared, all they'd planned, she went to Gio in secret? Why? Naomi was *his*. They were building a damn life here. Didn't that mean anything? He had half a thought to drive to Houston, hunt down this Gio and beat his face to a pulp. But as satisfying as that would be, it wouldn't change the fact that Naomi had sneaked off to meet him.

Toby needed time to think. Space to do it in. Slamming out of the workshop, he stalked to the stables and saddled a horse. It'd be best for all involved if he wasn't at the ranch when she came back.

Because he wasn't sure how he would handle it if she looked him dead in the eye and lied to him. Again.

Good thing he wasn't in love with her—or this would be killing him.

Astride the big black stallion, Toby headed out, and the horse's hooves beat out a rhythm that seemed to chant, *it's over, it's over, it's over...*

By the time Naomi made it home to the ranch, her anger at Gio had dissipated and she felt as if she was thinking clearly for the first time in days.

It was time to stand up to all the men in her life. She'd sent Gio packing, and heck, maybe she'd scare Toby into taking off, too. But she was tired of pretending, living a half life.

She was in love with Toby McKittrick, and today she was going to tell him just how lucky he was to have her. She didn't care if he wasn't in love with her right now. Naomi could wait. Because he loved her for who she was, and that was enough for her—for now. She had no doubt that he would come to feel the same way she did. He was only protecting himself after what Sasha had done to him. Hardly surprising that he would keep his heart safe after having it crushed by betrayal.

But she was going to show him that love didn't have to be about pain. And she would *make* him listen.

She steered her car into the long, curved drive toward the ranch house and realized that in the past few weeks, Paradise Ranch really had become home. Her heart was here. In the wide-open spaces. In the stupid chicken coop and with Legend, lying buried under a live oak at the rear of the property.

Her heart was with the man who had always been her friend and was now her lover. The man who had offered to be a father to her child. How could she *not* love him and everything they'd found together?

She didn't need Hollywood. She didn't need dreams of fame and fortune. She didn't even need her parents' approval anymore. All she needed was Toby.

When she parked the car, Naomi raced into the house, calling for him as she went from room to room. She'd been longer than she'd planned and so she expected him to be in his office, as he was most afternoons, working on plans for another amazing invention. But he wasn't there, so she headed to the kitchen and tried not to hear how the heels of her shoes sounded like a frantic heartbeat against the wood floors. "Toby?"

"He's not here," Rebecca said, poking her head into the room from the walk-in pantry. "Took off on that big black of his a few hours ago. Haven't seen him since."

Disappointed, Naomi asked, "Do you know where he went?"

"Nope." Rebecca shook her head, then went back to whatever she'd been doing before. "He took off like a bat outta hell, though. Must be something bothering him."

Worry replaced disappointment, and Naomi chewed at her bottom lip. What could have happened while she was gone? "Okay, thanks. Um, I'll try his cell."

"Phones on horses," Rebecca muttered. "It's a weird damn world..."

Naomi called him as soon as she was in the great room, and she listened to the ring go on and on until finally his voice mail activated. She didn't leave a message, just hung up. And as she looked out the window at the sprawl of the ranch she considered home, she wondered where he'd gone. And why.

An hour later, Toby opened the front door and stalked into the house.

She'd tried to reach him a dozen times, but his phone went to voice mail and her texts to him went unanswered. By the time she heard him enter the house, Naomi's nerves were strung so tightly she could have played a tune on them.

She followed the sound of his footsteps and found him in his office, pouring scotch into a heavy crystal tumbler. He glanced at her when she walked into the room, but there was no welcome on his face.

"Toby? Is everything okay?"

"Interesting question," he said without answering at all.

The only light in the room came from the dying sun drifting through the wide windows at his back. He was a shadow against the light, and even at that, she saw the tightness on his features, the hard gleam in his eyes. And she wondered.

"I was worried," she said, walking a little closer.

"Yeah?" He laughed shortly, took a long drink of scotch and said, "Me too. So, did you find some great wedding stuff in Houston?"

"Actually, that's what I wanted to talk to you about."

"Is that right?" His hand tightened around the glass, and even at a distance, she could see his knuckles whiten.

"I didn't really go to the city to shop."

He snapped his gaze to hers. "Yeah, I know. See, you weren't the only one texting me today."

"What do you mean?" Worry curled in the pit of her stomach and sent long, snaking tendrils spiraling through her bloodstream.

He pulled his phone from his pocket and held it out to her. "Here. Tell me what you think."

Naomi suddenly didn't want to know what was on his phone. What had made his eyes so cold and his mouth so relentlessly grim. But she forced herself to walk to him, take the phone and turn it on. The photo was already keyed up.

She and Gio at their shadowy table, leaning toward each other, his hand covering hers. They looked…cozy. Intimate. If she didn't know what had happened between them, she might believe that they were lovers, intensely focused on only each other.

Oh, God. What he must have thought when he saw this. She took a breath, looked up at him. "Toby—"

"You lied to me." His features were colder, harder than she'd ever seen them. Even when Sasha left him, he hadn't looked this closed off. Untouchable.

"I didn't lie."

"Semantics. By not telling me you were meeting Gio, you lied to me," he ground out through gritted teeth. "Damn it, Naomi."

He whirled around and threw the glass tumbler into the empty fireplace, where it shattered, sounding like the end of the world. Despite the heat of that action, Toby was coldly furious. When he whipped around to look at her, his sea-blue eyes were stormy and glinting with banked fury. "You're meeting Gio behind my back?"

"It wasn't like that."

"Really?" He pushed both hands through his hair. "Because that's just what it looks like in that picture. Maverick said I'm a fool, and I'm starting to think he's right."

Stunned, she stared at him. "Until now, Maverick was a lowlife. Now you're ready to take his ugliness over what I'm trying to tell you?" She took a step toward him. She hated that he stepped back, keeping her at bay. "Gio texted me. Said it was important that I meet him. So I went there to tell him to leave me alone."

"Yeah?" He cocked his head and gave her a sour

smile. "You needed a quiet little romantic corner to do that?"

"It wasn't romantic, Toby." She couldn't believe she was having to explain this. And wanted to kick herself for keeping it from him in the first place. "I don't want Gio. I want you."

"What's the matter? Gio not interested? Or, hey, maybe you're going to keep us both dangling. Is that the plan?" He shook his head and said, "Don't bother answering that. I don't need another lie."

"I'm not lying to you," she countered. God, she'd handled this all wrong. She should have gone to him, asked him to go to Houston with her. To face down Gio together. Instead, she'd wanted to clean up her own mess, and now it looked as though she'd simply traded one bad situation for a worse one. How could she make him see? Make him understand that he was wrong about all this?

Then she realized what she had to do. What she should have done weeks ago when she'd first admitted the truth to herself. "Toby, I love you."

He laughed, but the sound was harsh, strained, as if it had scraped along his throat like knives. "God, Naomi, don't. You really think telling me that is going to convince me?"

Stung, she swallowed the ache and demanded, "Well, what will?"

"Nothing," he said, staring at her as if she were a stranger.

Naomi's heart hurt, and her breath was strangled

in her lungs. She was losing everything and didn't know how to stop it. Toby's gaze was locked with hers, and through her pain, Naomi realized that she wasn't just hurt, she was *insulted*. She was closer to him than to anyone she'd ever known. He *knew* her and he was still going to take Maverick's word over hers?

She had to reach him. Had to fight for what they had, because if she gave up now, he'd never believe in her. Never accept that she loved him.

"You know me, Toby," she said and saw his eyes flash.

"Thought I did," he acknowledged.

"Well, thanks for the benefit of the doubt." She crossed her arms over her chest and hugged herself for comfort.

"What doubt? That picture says it all," he said.

"That picture says just what Maverick wanted it to say," she countered. His eyes were shuttered, his mouth tight and grim, and every inch of his tall, muscular body looked rigid with tension. She wasn't reaching him and she knew why. This wasn't Maverick and his nasty tricks. This went back much farther than that.

"This all comes back to Sasha," she said tightly.

"It has nothing to do with her." Toby stalked across the room, as if he needed some distance from her. As if shutting her out wasn't enough. Then he turned around to face Naomi. "She's gone. Been gone for years."

"And she took your heart with her," Naomi said, though it cost her to admit it.

"Please." He snorted.

"I'm not saying you're still in love with her," she said, voice cold as steel. "I'm saying that the part of you that was willing to trust, to take a risk, left with her. You loved her, and she walked out."

"I don't need the recap," he said. "I was there."

"Yes, me too," she reminded him. "I was there for you. I saw what you did to yourself to get past her. You closed off a part of your heart. Your soul. You didn't want to trust anyone because you were afraid to be hurt again."

"Afraid? I'm not afraid."

"Come on, Toby," she said. "At least be honest."

"Oh, like you?" he asked with a snort of derisive laughter.

She winced, because even she knew she'd had that shot coming.

"Today was the first time I've ever lied to you, Toby, and I didn't like it. You know me. So whatever it is you're feeling right now isn't about me meeting with Gio."

"Is that so? Then what is it about, Naomi?"

"It's about you using Maverick's photo as an excuse to back away from me before I get too close."

If anything, his features tightened even further. "That's bull."

"Is it?" She stomped across the room, stopped right in front of him, tipped her head back and

looked into his dark, angry eyes. "I didn't do anything wrong. Well, okay," she admitted, "I should
have told you that I was meeting Gio today."

"Yeah, I'd say so."

"But," she continued as if he hadn't spoken at all,
"other than that, I've done nothing to earn your mis-
trust, Toby. You're my friend. My lover. The man I
trust to be a father to my baby."

A muscle in his jaw twitched furiously, but he
didn't speak. That was fine by Naomi, because she
wasn't finished.

"Sasha hurt you so badly you don't trust anybody."

"I trusted you," he said quietly. "Look where that
got me."

"You didn't. Not really." Funny, she was only just
seeing it now. "You've been holding back all along.
Waiting for something to go wrong. For me to screw
up. To prove to you that I was no better than Sasha."

"Not true."

"Of course it's true," she snapped. "My mistake
was playing into it. I was afraid to tell you how I really felt because I thought you'd shut me out even
more if you knew."

His eyes narrowed. "Knew what?"

"I should have told you in California, when I realized it for the first time," she admitted. "I *love* you,
Toby. I'm *in* love with you."

"I don't want to hear this."

"Too bad," she said. "You need to." Naomi shook

her head and stared up into his eyes, willing him to see the truth. "I'm not going to pretend anymore. I love you. If you don't believe me, I can't do anything about that.

"But I knew you'd react this way, and that's why I didn't tell you. I thought I could wait, that you would eventually come to love me back." She cupped his face in her palms and held on when he would have shaken her off. "I'm not so sure of that now, and you know what? I'm not going to wait for crumbs, Toby. I deserve more. We both do. I can't be with someone who doesn't trust me. Doesn't believe in me. Doesn't love me."

Turning around, she walked to the door, hoping with every step that he would stop her. Ask her to stay. But it didn't happen, and disappointment welled up inside her until it dripped from her eyes.

She paused briefly at the threshold to look back at him. So tall, so strong, so determined to cut himself off from love. Sadly, Naomi told herself she had nothing to gain by staying except more pain—and she'd had enough of that for one day.

"Congratulations, Toby," she said sadly. "You found a way out of this marriage, and you convinced yourself it was my fault. A win-win for you, right? You're using my stupid meeting with Gio as your excuse to not have to feel. It's easier that way. If you hold yourself back, you don't risk anything."

"Why did you meet Gio, then?"

She smiled sadly. "You should have just asked me

that first, Toby. You should have trusted me. Believed
in me. But you didn't. This marriage was a bargain.
An act. But that's not enough for me anymore. I
want it all. Or I don't want any of it. I deserve more.
So does my baby." She took a breath and let it out.
"Toby, so do you."

She didn't wait for an answer. Instead, she walked
out, grabbed her purse off the hall tree in the entryway, then left the ranch, closing the door quietly
behind her.

Eleven

"She's right, you know."

Toby looked over at his sister as she gave one of his pregnant mares a checkup. "Figures you'd say that. You're female."

Scarlett bit back a smile. "True, females are far more logical than males, but even a man should be able to see the truth here. You're just not letting yourself."

Why the hell had he talked to Scarlett about this? Answer? He hadn't slept, and he'd been on edge since the day before, when Naomi walked out, left him standing in his office, more alone than he'd ever been in his life. Temper still spiking, he'd roamed through his house like a ghost, haunting every room, seeing Naomi wherever he looked. Maybe *she* was the ghost, he corrected silently.

Either way, he felt like his head was going to explode with all the thoughts running through it. Then Scarlett had shown up, and he'd blurted it all out before he could stop himself. He and his sister had always been close. He'd expected some support. Instead, he was getting his ass kicked. Figuratively speaking.

Stubbornly, though, he reminded his sister, "She went into Houston to meet that sleaze Gio and didn't bother to tell me."

"Did you give her a chance to when you came home?" Scarlett asked. "Or did you just jump down her throat with accusations?"

He frowned and asked himself when Scarlett's loyalties had shifted to Naomi. Female solidarity? Made a man feel like he was standing outside, pounding on a door for someone to notice him.

When he didn't answer, Scarlett said, "Yeah, that's what I thought."

"I saw the picture, Scarlett," he argued, remembering that hard punch to the gut that had hit him when he first saw the photo Maverick had sent him.

"You saw exactly what that bastard Maverick wanted you to see," she corrected.

He looked at her and waited, because he knew she wasn't finished.

"Damn it, Toby, that guy's been creating chaos all over Royal for months and you know it." She smoothed her hands up and down the mare's foreleg to make sure the strain she'd suffered a few days before was healing well. When Scarlett stood up again, she said, "You reacted just the way he wanted you to. My God, could you be any more predictable?"

That was irritating, so he didn't address it. "Maverick's been hitting people with *truth*, hasn't he?"

"Uh-huh. The truth was, she met with Gio. She didn't fling herself at him and run off to the closest hotel room. You're the one who filled in that blank."

He scowled at her, but she didn't stop.

"And you know, Maverick hit Naomi with truth and you stood by her." Tipping her head to one side, she stepped around the mare, running her hand across the animal's back as she moved. "You think maybe Maverick might have been ticked that she didn't fall apart? That her life wasn't ruined by his vicious little attack? You think it bothered the hell out of him that you went riding to the rescue?"

He scrubbed one hand across his jaw. His brain started working even through the sleep-deprived fog, and he had to admit that she might have a point. "Maybe."

"Uh-huh. And maybe he was mad enough to go after *you* this time? To get you to turn from Naomi so she could be as crushed as he'd planned in the first place?" She leaned her forearms on the stall's half door and looked up at him. "And then *you*, being male and not exactly logical when it comes to the women in your life, react just like he wanted you to."

Well, if any of that was true, it was damned annoying. Toby hated the thought that he'd done just what Maverick had wanted him to do. Hated being that predictable. He remembered the look in Naomi's eyes and wondered if Scarlett was onto something. Had his sister instantly understood something that he'd been too blind to see? Then Scarlett started talking again, and he was feeling less magnanimous toward her.

"Naomi was right about you and Sasha."

He shot her a single, hard look. "Leave it alone."

"Yeah, that's gonna happen," she said with a laugh as she swung her hair back from her face. "You know Mom and I were worried about you when Sasha took off."

He did know that, and it didn't make him feel any better to recognize it. Sure, he'd taken it hard, but anyone would have. He remembered his family trying to make him see that Sasha leaving was the best thing that could've happened to him. But he hadn't been willing to admit that then.

"Yeah, so?"

"Naomi was the one you turned to back then."

"I know that, too." He remembered how Naomi had drawn him out of the dark fury that had held him in a grip for weeks after the woman he thought he'd loved left with another man. She'd stuck by him no matter what he'd done to make her leave. She'd stayed to be insulted when he was rude to her.

Naomi had just flat refused to leave him alone to

brood. Instead, she'd dragged him out to the mov-
ies, to dinner, to picnics. He'd remembered how to
laugh because of her. And eventually, he'd admitted
that it hadn't been Sasha he had missed, but the idea
of her. Of a wife. Family.

"But you're still holding on to what Sasha made
you feel, Toby."

"The hell I am." He brushed that aside, stepped
back and opened the stall door so his sister could
exit. When she was out, he closed and locked the
door behind her.

Sunlight speared through the open stable door to
form a slash of pale gold along the center aisle. The
scent of hay and horses was thick in the air, but it
didn't give Toby the sense of peace it usually did.
Hell, there was never peace when Scarlett was on
a tear.

"You don't even realize it," his sister said, "but
ever since that woman, you've looked at everyone
else like you're just waiting for them to turn on you.
To prove themselves dishonest. Untrustworthy."

He shifted uneasily. He was long since over Sasha,
but the lesson she'd taught him had remained fresh.
"So being cautious is wrong?"

"That's not cautious, Toby," she said, laying one
hand on his chest. "That's cowardly."

"Oh, thanks very much." He turned and headed
for the next stall, opening it for her and holding it
even when she didn't step inside.

"What would you call it if someone refused to

care again because they might get hurt? Refused to trust again because they might be let down?"

He wanted to say careful, but he was afraid she had a point.

"Naomi loves you."

"How the hell do you know that?" he demanded. "She only told *me* last night."

"And you let her leave anyway?" Scarlett's eyes went wide in astonishment. "God, you really are an idiot. Of course she loves you. She always has. If you weren't such a stubborn *male*, you would have noticed it on your own."

She walked into the stall and slammed the door closed behind her.

"Love wasn't part of our deal," he argued, even knowing it was weak.

"Love isn't a bargain, Toby. It's a gift. One you just returned." She shook her head again and turned away to do another physical on the next mare. "Idiot."

Toby watched her but stopped listening to her frustrated muttering. He had a feeling it wasn't real flattering to him anyway. And maybe he didn't deserve flattery. Maybe he was the idiot his sister had called him.

And maybe, he thought in disgust, he'd tossed aside something he should have been fighting for.

When her cell phone rang, Naomi grabbed it, hoping to see Toby's name on her screen, and felt a swift stab of disappointment when it wasn't him. She answered on a sigh. "Hi, Cecelia."

Her friend started talking in a rush. "Naomi, you remember that guy Gio you told me and Simone about when you came home from that big fashion show?"

Naomi rolled her eyes and dropped into a chair. Curling her feet up underneath her, she said wryly, "Yes, I remember him." *Just saw him yesterday*, she wanted to add but didn't. "What about him?"

"I was watching that gossip channel on cable just now, and he's all over it." Cecelia paused for dramatic effect. "Can I just say wow? You didn't tell us how pretty he is."

"He's not that good-looking in person," Naomi assured her. Especially, she added silently, when you added in his personality. His character. Compared to Toby, Gio Fabiani was simply an attractive waste of space.

"Well, he looks good on camera," Cecelia said. "Except he's not looking real happy right now."

Naomi sighed again. She was tired, since she'd been up half the night reliving that argument with Toby. And the other half of the night, her dream self had done the same thing.

This morning, she'd been on the phone handling dozens of things, all the while letting the back of her mind work on what she would say to Toby when she talked to him again. Because they *were* going to talk. She wasn't going to let him end what they'd just so recently found because of a stupid lie. Should she have told him about meeting Gio? Sure. In hindsight, it was perfectly clear. But at the time, she'd been trying to handle things on her own. Clear up her past and set up her future. Why was that so hard to understand?

Resting her head against the back of the chair, she stared up at the ceiling and asked listlessly, "Why's he on the news?"

"Get this," Cecelia said, clearly settling in for a good gossip session. "There are *three* different women suing him for child support."

Surprised, but somehow comforted by the fact that she wasn't the only foolish woman to have landed in Gio's bed, Naomi chuckled a little to herself. "Really?"

"Oh, yeah, apparently it's huge news in Italy. He even left the country to get out of the spotlight for a while."

"If he's on the news, doesn't sound like that plan worked."

"I know, right? And you know what's weird?" Cecelia asked, and didn't wait for an answer. "Some photographer caught him at the airport in Houston. He was running to catch a plane headed to England. He was right here in Texas. Can you believe it?"

And now he was gone, Naomi thought with a pleased smile. Obviously, he'd taken what she said to heart and wasn't waiting around to see if she'd change her mind. "Well, I hope those women catch up to him."

"I think they will," Cecelia said. "He's got to go home sometime, right? Anyway, I just thought it was weird, seeing him on TV and knowing you'd met him—"

"It is weird." Beyond weird. But it explained why Gio had been desperate enough for money to give extortion a try. The upside here was, with three other women and children to worry about, the man would certainly be willing to sign over his parental rights, so that was good for Naomi and her baby.

Cecelia was talking, but Naomi was only half listening. Instead, she was thinking about Toby. Maybe she should have stayed at the ranch last night and just had it out with him. But he'd hurt her, damn it. Hurt her by dismissing her when she told him she loved him. It had been a big moment for her, opening herself up like that, and he hadn't believed her.

Hadn't trusted her, and that, she thought, hurt most of all. He'd been waiting, or so it seemed to her, for Naomi to let him down. To prove that what they had couldn't be counted on. Scowling, she thought about the night before, and then something dawned on her.

A part of his mind and heart had been convinced that she would leave him. Walk away. To protect himself, he'd held back, committing to a marriage he didn't believe would work so that when it failed, he wasn't blindsided by it.

With a jolt, Naomi sat up straight. And what had she done? Walked away in the middle of an argument. She'd walked away. Just as he'd expected her to do. "Oh, God."

"Naomi, are you even listening to me?"

She winced. "Sorry, Cec, I'm just really distracted."

"Everything okay with you and Toby?"

She hesitated and almost lied but didn't want to get into the habit, so she said only, "It will be. We're just working out a few things."

Like our lives.

"Oh, I totally get it. Between weddings and babies and the rush of hormones…we're all half-crazed these days. I'll let you go, sweetie. I just wanted to tell you about that Gio guy."

"And I appreciate the update," Naomi said. "We'll talk soon."

When the call ended, she stood up and walked through the condo, realizing that this wasn't her place anymore. Her place was with Toby. Whether he knew it or not.

Grimly, she turned her phone on and made a call. When a woman answered, she said, "Scarlett, this is Naomi. Where's your brother?"

"An hour ago, he was at the ranch, and he was pretty damn crabby, too."

Naomi smiled. "He's about to get a lot crabbier."

"Yay!"

Naomi drove straight to the ranch, telling herself if he wasn't there, she'd wait. She wasn't going to leave again without making him see the truth of what they had. What they *could* have. And if she'd just stayed right there last night, they'd be through this already. *Mental note: no more walking out.*

Her hair twisted wildly in the wind blasting through her open window. The Texas summer sky was a brassy blue with only a few stray clouds drifting aimlessly, looking lost and alone in that vast expanse. There was no traffic on the road, so she pushed the car as fast as she dared. The baby was moving around excitedly, almost as if he or she knew they were headed home. Naomi smiled fiercely and caught her own eye in the rearview mirror.

She was going to make Toby listen. Make him believe. Make him love her as much as she loved him. Naomi had waited for love her whole life, and she wasn't going to settle for less.

Gravel flew up from behind her tires as she took the long drive to the ranch. Her gaze swept the familiar, looking for Toby, and then she spotted him, getting into his truck.

"Oh, no," she murmured, "you're not leaving yet." She pulled to a stop directly in front of the truck, blocking him from leaving. Then she threw the gear into Park, jumped out and walked toward him with long, determined strides.

Toby's breath caught in his throat. When he saw her car flying down the drive, he thought he'd never seen anything that beautiful. She was coming home on her own. But now, watching the woman who held his heart, he had to admit that she looked both gorgeous…and dangerous. There was fire in her eye, and what did it say about him that he found that damned sexy?

It was so good to see her. To catch her scent on the wind. He wanted to tangle his hands in that thick hair of hers, slant his mouth over hers and feel that rush of *rightness* that always went through him when they were together.

Since she walked out the door yesterday, he'd felt only half-alive. Through his anger and pain, there was a constant ache for her. In spite of distrusting her, he wanted her. In spite of everything, he'd missed her.

And after talking to Scarlett today, he'd realized that he'd handled that talk with Naomi all wrong. He hadn't even listened to her, because he'd been so wrapped up in the surety that he'd been right to keep his heart locked away.

But he was wrong. About all of it. And it was long past time she heard everything he'd been keeping inside.

"You're not leaving, Toby," she said when she was close enough.

"No need to now," he said affably, one corner of his mouth lifting as her eyes spit fire at him.

"Not until we get a few things straight," she said, then asked, "What did you say?"

"I was coming to you, Naomi, so, no," he said, "I'm not going anywhere now."

Some of that temper that had been driving her melted away. He could see it in the way her shoulders relaxed some. "You were really coming to me?"

"Couldn't take the silence here, Naomi. The emptiness. I needed you to come home. And you have."

He grabbed hold of her, yanked her in close and kissed her, letting his body tell her everything that was so hard to say in words. She leaned into him, and he felt whole for the first time in hours. This was where he belonged. Right here, with her. The world righted itself, and every last, lingering doubt hiding in the shadows of his mind dissolved in the realization of what he had—what he had almost lost.

When he finally lifted his head, he looked down into her eyes and said, "I'm sorry."

"Excuse me? You're sorry?"

He grinned a little. "Is it so surprising?"

"Well," she admitted, "yes. I didn't expect you to say that. I thought we'd finish our argument and that I'd have to hold you down to make you listen to me. An apology wasn't in the game plan."

"I was wrong, Naomi. Expected or not, I am sorry. I never should have let Maverick get to me." He released her, jammed his hands in the back pockets of his jeans and admitted, "I reacted just the way he wanted me to. I shut you down. Wouldn't listen. Hell, I didn't even listen to myself, because of course I trust you, Naomi."

She blew out a breath, then pressed her lips together in an attempt to steady herself. Toby knew her even better than he knew himself, and that was just one more reason why he'd been the idiot his sister had called him.

Naomi didn't cheat. Naomi would never hurt him.

"Thanks for that," she said and gave him a tremulous smile.

"I saw that picture and I lost it," he admitted, jerking his hands free and tossing them in the air helplessly. "I didn't think. Didn't remember that the bastard's whole point is to create chaos and tear people apart."

"It wouldn't have done anything to us if I had just told you about Gio wanting to meet with me in the first place, Toby." Her eyes were shining as she looked up at him. "I should have asked you to go with me."

Watching her, he asked what he should have the day before. "Why didn't you?"

"Because I wanted to handle it myself." She laid both hands on the curve of the baby and rubbed, as if soothing the child within. "I wanted to kick him out of my life, *our* lives. Once I was there, I was wishing for you, though, if that helps."

"A little," he admitted. "I get you wanting to do it yourself, Naomi. But you could have told me."

"And should have, I know." She pushed her hand through her wind-tangled hair and sighed. "He wanted money. Threatened to tell the world that he's my baby's father if I didn't pay him off."

Toby felt a hard punch of anger and gritted his

teeth against the helpless flood of it. He really wished he had five minutes alone with the man. "What did you say to that?"

"I told him to go ahead. It would make it easier to sue him for child support."

A laugh shot from Toby's throat. "You did?"

"Yes, and he wasn't happy," she said, smiling now. "But according to Cecelia, he's got bigger problems at the moment."

"What?"

"Not important," she said, shaking her head. "I'll tell you later. Toby. Why were you coming to see me?"

"Because sometime between last night and this morning, I finally figured something out." He reached for her again, laid both hands on her shoulders and held on. "I was coming to tell you that I love you, Naomi."

She gasped and clapped one hand to her mouth. Her eyes filled instantly with a sheen of tears. "Really?"

"Yes." His gaze moved over her face, taking in every detail. In the sunlight, the bright streaks in her hair shone like polished copper. Behind her hand, her mouth was curved in a small smile, as if she wanted to believe him but couldn't quite manage it. And her eyes, her beautiful eyes glittered with love and hope.

"I love you, Naomi," he said again, willing her to trust him. To believe him. "I was a jackass yesterday. I was so worried about losing you I forgot to fight to keep you."

"Toby…"

He had no clue what she was going to say, but Toby was determined to speak first. To tell her everything he should have told her when he first suggested they get married.

"I shouldn't have shut down like that yesterday. I do trust you, Naomi. It was my own stubbornness that didn't let me tell you that I think I've always loved you." He ran his hands up and down her arms, kept his gaze locked with hers. "I'm lucky enough to be in love with my best friend."

She pressed her lips together and reached up to impatiently swipe tears from her eyes. "When I left yesterday, Toby, I wasn't really *leaving*, you know. I always planned to come back."

"You walking away is something I never want to see again, Naomi. Don't think I could take it." Just the thought of losing her was enough to bring him to his knees.

When Sasha left, anger had driven him. If he lost Naomi, he'd lose his soul.

"You don't have to worry about that," she assured him, stepping in to wrap her arms around his waist. "I'm not going anywhere. I'm exactly where I want to be."

He held on to her for several long minutes, relishing the beat of her heart against his chest, the scent of her shampoo flavoring every breath and the thump of their child, kicking to get attention.

Finally, though, he pulled back, caged her face between his palms and said, "I want to adopt your baby, Naomi. As soon as it's born, I want to be its father. So that baby will never doubt that he or she belongs. That we're family."

"Oh, Toby…" Tears trickled down her cheeks, but she smiled through them, and his heart turned over to see the love beaming in her eyes.

"And about the California thing," Toby added quickly, wanting to say it all now while he was holding her close. "If you have to be there for weeks on end to tape your show, we'll manage. We can buy a house in the hills there and we'll have a California base for whenever we need it."

"You'd do that for me?" she asked.

"For *us*," he corrected, wiping her tears away with his thumbs.

"It means so much to me that you would," Naomi said and went up on her toes to kiss him, hard and fast. "But you don't have to. I called Tamara today to tell her thanks but no, thanks."

Now it was his turn to be surprised. "What? Why would you do that?"

"Because I don't need it in the desperate way I used to," she said. "Before, I wanted my show to succeed so badly so I could prove myself. To my parents. To myself. Because the show was all I had, I poured everything into it.

"But these past few weeks, I've discovered I'm more than my show, Toby. I don't need to make a point. I need you. *Us*."

"But, Naomi, this was your dream."

She shrugged and smiled. "If Tamara Stiles can

get *Fashion Sense* on stations around the country, so can I. And doing it myself means it gets done my way. I don't have to leave Texas, leave what makes my show what it is to make it succeed. I'll get there. It'll just take a little longer."

"You're amazing," he said quietly. He'd always seen her strength, and he was glad she could see it now, too. "I believe in you, Naomi. You wait and see. In a few years, your show is going to put Royal on the map."

She grinned. "As long as you're with me, then everything will be perfect."

"Oh, I'm with you, honey. And you'll never shake me loose now."

"Good to hear," she said and moved to kiss him again.

He stopped her cold with a shake of his head. "Not yet. We've got something else to settle first."

"What's left?" she asked, but she was smiling and he was grateful. He never wanted to see her cry again.

"Just this." Toby went down on one knee in front of her and pulled a simply set sapphire ring from his pocket. Holding it up, he saw more tears and told himself this one last time was okay. "You didn't want an engagement ring before because it wouldn't have been real. I hope you'll take this one, though. This ring belonged to my grandmother, Naomi. It symbolizes the fifty years of love she and my grandpa shared."

"Toby…"

His gaze locked on hers, Toby said softly, "I'm offering you this ring, Naomi. I want to give you my name, my love and the future we'll build together. Marry me for real, Naomi. Trust me with your heart, with your baby. Give me more babies. Fill this big empty house with the kind of love that lasts generations."

"Oh, Toby, my heart hurts it's so full," she whispered brokenly.

"That's a yes, then?"

"Yes, of course it's yes."

He slid the ring onto her finger, where that cool sapphire caught the sunlight and winked up at both of them. Then he lifted the hem of her shirt and pressed a gentle kiss to the mound of her belly and heard her sigh as she stroked her fingers through his hair.

Then he stood up and looked into her eyes as he pulled her into his arms. "I love you, Naomi," he whispered. "Always have. Always will."

She sighed again, smiled and lifted one hand to smooth his hair back from his forehead. "I love you, Toby. Always have. Always will."

"Good to hear," he said, lowering his head for a kiss.

Naomi grinned. "Talk, talk, talk. Show me what you've got, cowboy."

He grinned back, and then he showed her.

* * * * *

COMING NEXT MONTH FROM

HARLEQUIN *Desire*

Available July 3, 2017

#2527 THE BABY FAVOR

Billionaires and Babies • by Andrea Laurence

CEO Mason Spencer and his wife are headed for divorce when an old promise changes their plans. They are now the guardians for Spencer's niece...and they must remain married. Will this be their second chance, one that leads to forever?

#2528 LONE STAR BABY SCANDAL

Texas Cattleman's Club: Blackmail • by Lauren Canan

When sexy former rodeo champion turned billionaire Clay Everett sets his sights on his spunky secretary, he's sure he holds the reins in their affair. Until he learns Sophie Prescott is carrying his child. Now all bets are off!

#2529 HIS UNEXPECTED HEIR

Little Secrets • by Maureen Child

After a fling with a sexy marine leaves Rita pregnant, her attempts to reach the billionaire are met with silence...until now! Brooding, reclusive Jack offers to marry Rita—in name only. Will his new family give him the heart to embrace life—and love—again?

#2530 PREGNANT BY THE BILLIONAIRE

The Locke Legacy • by Karen Booth

Billionaire Sawyer Locke only makes commitments to his hotel empire—until he meets fiery PR exec Kendall Ross. Now he can't get her out of his mind—or out of his bed. But when she becomes pregnant, will he claim the heir he never expected?

#2531 BEST FRIEND BRIDE

In Name Only • by Kat Cantrell

CEO Jonas Kim must stop his arranged marriage—by arranging a marriage for himself! His best friend, Vivian, will be his wife and never fall in love, or so he thinks. Can he keep his heart safe when Viv tempts him to become friends with benefits?

#2532 CLAIMING THE COWGIRL'S BABY

Red Dirt Royalty • by Silver James

Rancher Kaden inherited a birth father, a powerful last name and wealth—none of which he wants. His pregnant lover, debutante Pippa Duncan, has lost everything due to a dark family secret. Their marriage of convenience may undo the pain of their families' pasts, but will it lead to love?

Get 2 Free Books,

Plus 2 Free Gifts—

HARLEQUIN *Desire*

just for trying the Reader Service!

Jack didn't make a habit of coming here. Memories were
thick and he tended to avoid them, because remembering
wouldn't get him a damn thing. But against his will, images
filled his mind.

Every damn moment of that time with Rita was etched
into his brain in living, vibrant color. He could hear the
sound of her voice. The music of her laughter. He saw the
shine in her eyes and felt the silk of her touch.

"And you've been working for months to forget it," he
reminded himself in a mutter. "No point in dredging it up
now."

What they'd found together all those months ago was
over. There was no going back. He'd made a promise to
himself. One he intended to keep.

It was a hard lesson to learn, but he had learned it in the
hot, dry sands of a distant country. And that lesson haunted
him to this day.

But Jack Buchanan didn't surrender to the dregs of fear, so he kept walking, made himself notice the everyday world pulsing around him. Along the street, a pair of musicians was playing for the crowd and the dollar bills tossed into an open guitar case. Shop owners had tables set up outside their storefronts to entice customers and, farther down the street, a line snaked from a bakery's doors all along the sidewalk.

He hadn't been downtown in months, so he'd never seen the bakery before. Apparently, though, it had quite the loyal customer base. Dozens of people—from teenagers to career men and women—waited patiently to get through the open bakery door. As he got closer, amazing scents wafted through the air and he understood the crowds gathering. Idly, Jack glanced through the wide, shining front window at the throng within, then stopped dead as an all-too-familiar laugh drifted to him.

Everything inside Jack went cold and still. He hadn't heard that laughter in months, but he'd have known it anywhere. Throaty, rich, it made him think of long hot nights, silk sheets and big brown eyes staring up into his in the darkness.

He'd tried to forget her. Had, he'd thought, buried the memories; yet now they came roaring back, swamping him until Jack had to fight for breath.

Even as he told himself it couldn't be her, Jack was bypassing the line and stalking into the bakery.

HARLEQUIN® *Desire*

AVAILABLE JULY 2017

LONE STAR BABY SCANDAL

BY

LAUREN CANAN

PART OF THE SIZZLING
TEXAS CATTLEMAN'S CLUB: BLACKMAIL SERIES

When sexy former rodeo champion turned billionaire Clay Everett
sets his sights on his spunky secretary, he's sure he holds the reins
in their affair. Until he learns Sophie Prescott is carrying his child.
Now all bets are off!

AND DON'T MISS A SINGLE INSTALLMENT OF

BLACKMAIL

No secret—or heart—is safe in Royal, Texas...